I0554180

Thunder, Mist, and Frost

Thunder, Mist, and Frost

Frost

Nature's Fury and Delights

LEENIE BROWN

LEENIE B BOOKS
HALIFAX

No part of this book may be reproduced in any form, except in the case of brief quotations embodied in critical articles or reviews, without written permission from its publisher and author.

This book is a work of fiction. All names, events, and places are a product of this author's imagination. If any name, event and/or place did exist, it is purely by coincidence that it appears in this book.

Cover design by Leenie B Books. Images sourced from DepositPhotos and PeriodImages.

Nature's Fury and Delights: Thunder, Mist, and Frost © 2018 Leenie Brown. All Rights Reserved, except where otherwise noted.

Contents

Frosted Windowpanes

Dear Reader,

Welcome!

I am delighted to share the first three thirty-minute reads in my new *Nature's Fury and Delights Collection* with you. These stories will always feature some element of nature and a sweet romance, but how those things get woven together and with which main characters will constantly be changing. I hope that these novelettes will give you as much pleasure in reading them as I had while creating them for you.

Thunder

When the distant rumble of thunder forces Darcy to seek shelter from the coming storm, he finds much more than a refuge.

Chapter 1

As thunder rumbled in the distance, Fitzwilliam Darcy brushed a droplet of rain from his cheek and knew he needed to find shelter soon. Those heavy grey clouds were not going to hold their contents much longer. Indeed, the raindrop he had dashed from his cheek was a sign that a deluge was imminent.

He turned his horse toward a small copse of trees beyond which he knew stood a cottage. It was a small structure — one that was seldom used for anything other than an escape to solitude under the guise of hunting. There he would find materials for a fire, blankets, and a few easily kept supplies waiting for him, but, most importantly, that cottage would provide for him a refuge from the coming storm.

By the time Darcy swung down from his horse

and saw to the beast's care, the few drops of rain that had alerted him to danger had increased, and he knew he would do well to enter the cottage without being thoroughly drenched. Pulling his hat down, he ducked his head and raced to the cottage door, where he flung the door wide and entered rapidly, removing his hat from his head and shaking the rain from it as he did.

"Oh!" a shocked voice greeted him as he entered.

Darcy stopped what he was doing and stared for a moment at the pretty source of the surprised greeting. "Who are you?" he asked as he pushed the door closed.

The petite lady before him pulled herself straight, increasing her height by a full half inch, and lifted her chin. "Miss Elizabeth Bennet."

As Darcy took a long, silent look at Elizabeth, she shifted under his scrutiny, but just barely. From where he stood, she appeared to be a charming woman in a determined, unwavering sort of fashion. Her eyes were the colour of a clear summer day, her hair tumbled down her back in waves the colour of a strong cup of coffee, and her figure? Ah, her figure! What gentlemen would not admire a figure such as hers? Even covered from neck to toe in a sturdy brown pelisse, he could see that it was slight and exceedingly pleasing.

"And pray tell, Miss Bennet, how came you to be in my cottage?"

The brow over her left eye arched. "How came you to be so wet, sir?"

Darcy chuckled at her impertinence. "We call it rain here in the north. What do you call it in the south?" He could tell by her accent that she was not from the area.

Her lips twitched. "We call it precipitation when we wish to sound scholarly, or rain when we do not."

Clearly, she had a sharp wit and a sardonic sense of humour – two traits that Darcy found delightful. His mother had been similar when at home and not in company.

"Then, you are hiding from the rain as well?"

She gave a sharp nod of her head in reply and drew from behind her back a bonnet that looked as if it had been attacked by some angry maid with a broom.

"A branch," she said in explanation. "I had hoped to duck in here, repair what I could of my hat and hair, and wait out the storm before continuing my walk."

"Are you staying nearby?" Darcy removed his greatcoat and draped it over a chair next to the table upon which he had placed his hat.

"Have you a name?" she replied. "For I should like to know on whose property I am trespassing before I admit to more than my name. I should hate for my host to bear any reproach for my behaviour."

To Darcy, she did not appear to be anxious regarding her situation in the least. There was no nervous shifting of her feet or faltering in her speech. She spoke boldly as one who had not a worry in the world. In fact, the dancing light in her eyes seemed to say she already knew to whom she was speaking.

"And if I refuse to answer?" Darcy motioned to one of the two chairs before the hearth as an invitation for her to be seated while he went about the task of lighting a fire.

"Then I shall tell you no more than my name. As it is, I only need a few moments to repair this hat, and then I will be on my way." She perched on the edge of the chair to the right of the firebox and turned her attention to her bonnet.

Darcy sat back on his heels and stared at her incredulously. "You would venture out into that storm if I do not tell you my name? Did you not say you were going to wait out the storm in here?"

Her hands stilled, and she lifted puzzled eyes to him. "I entered this cottage unmarried and with a respectable reputation. I intend to leave it in a similar state whether you tell me your name or not." Her eyes and her hands returned to her work.

She was intent upon leaving? Did she lack sense? She had seemed intelligent up until now.

"You cannot go out into that storm. I cannot allow it."

"You cannot allow it?" Her voice was full of indignation. "You are nobody to me save a stranger, whose name I do not even know, and I will leave if I choose." She lifted her bonnet, tipped it one way and then another before resuming her repairs.

She was being foolish. Between the rain and the lightning mixed with the fog that often settled into this valley, she would be lost in moments after leaving the safety of this cottage.

"How well do you know the path?" He struck the flint against the steel over his tinderbox. Perhaps he could talk some sense into her – make her see reason and change her decision. No one would know she was here alone with him. To leave just to protect a reputation when leaving would put her life in danger was utter foolishness.

"I have walked it every day for the past six days."

He bent and blew on the glowing tinder, encouraging the fire to leap up and catch the small bit of kindling he held in his hand.

"And how many of those times were in the rain and fog?" he asked as he put the burning kindling into the firebox. The dampness would be soon driven out of the air in the cottage once the flames grew strong enough to devour a small log. Then, he would boil some water and make tea.

"There was fog yesterday." She lifted her hat once again for inspection.

Seeing her look of satisfaction, Darcy snatched the bonnet from her.

"My hat!" Elizabeth exclaimed as she grabbed for it.

Darcy placed it behind his back, so that she could not reach it. "The fog yesterday was light.

Today, with this rain, it will be heavy. You will not be able to see more than a few feet in front of you, which will make it far too easy for you to get turned around and find yourself facing a rocky precipice instead of the path to the Foleys' home."

He smiled as her mouth dropped open. "You bear a resemblance to Mrs. Foley when you are displeased."

"And have you seen my great aunt displeased very often, Mr. Darcy?" She folded her arm and glared at him.

He chuckled. Yes, he had seen that glare a few times in his life.

"More when I was younger and especially when my cousin was visiting, but it has been years. I do not feel the need to eat her apples any longer." He crossed the room and placed Elizabeth's bonnet near his hat on the table. "I should hate to see how angry she would be with me if she were to discover I allowed her niece to wander through a storm and fall to her death." He shook his head. "The bonnet and you are both remaining."

"And how angry do you think my aunt will be when she discovers I have spent an extended period of time in a cottage with a gentleman alone?"

He grabbed her wrist as she attempted to reach around him and retrieve her hat. The action drew her closer to him. Even at her full height she only came to his chin. "Do you still climb trees?"

Her look of anger faded from her eyes, and the scathing reproof he was certain she was about to unleash on him died on her lips.

"Do you," he repeated, "still ... climb trees?" Her nearness was causing his breath to quicken. He should let go of her wrist, but then she might snatch that bonnet and fly from the cottage.

"How do you know I used to climb trees?"

He shrugged and then, lifting her hand, turned it over to inspect her palm. "You have visited your aunt before, and you like apples."

Her hands were not so soft as some young ladies' hands were, but they were not so rough as those of his housekeeper or any of his maids. She must not toil with her hands. She must just thwart propriety. Her pelisse was made of good cloth, which also spoke to her status as higher than that of a tenant farmer's daughter.

He peeked at her sheepishly. "I believe it was

about three years ago when I watched someone, who very much resembled you, climb the apple tree near Mrs. Foley's kitchen. I was returning home from this very cottage. My father was staying here for two more days, but my mother wished to have me home for a time before I returned to school. I had intended to stop at your aunt's home and ask for an apple, but then I saw you."

Her brows were furrowed. "You were going to *ask* for an apple? Not take one?"

He shook his head. "I had learned my lesson about that a few years earlier. My father was even less pleased than your aunt when he heard about it. To be fair, she had warned my cousin and me that she would tell him if she ever caught us again. She is a woman of her word."

"As am I," Elizabeth pulled her hand from his grip and attempted once again to snatch her hat.

Without thinking, Darcy wrapped his arms around her to keep her from reaching the bonnet, but then quickly released her and, taking up her bonnet, stood across the table from her. "Forgive me. I was not thinking about anything but your safety."

11

Chapter 2

Darcy's instinct may have been focused on keeping her here safe, warm, and dry within this cottage when he wrapped his arms around her, but now, as he stood across from her with a table between them, those same instincts were causing him to question his own safety.

It was not that she posed some sort of danger to him physically. He certainly did not feel threatened. He did not expect her to snatch up the poker from the fire and attack him with it. Nor did he expect her to throw herself at him and pummel him into unconsciousness. His person, his physical being, was not in danger of injury. However, from the jolt of pleasure he had received when he wrapped his arms around her, he knew that he was in grave danger of being tortured by his desires, and that thought was excessively unsettling.

He had been attracted to many ladies in his several seasons in town. He had even, at one time, imagined himself in love with Miss Scott, whose father owned an estate no more than ten miles from his father's. Therefore, it was not as if he had never experienced the sensations of desire. He had, and yet until this moment, he had never feared those desires as he did now, for he had never felt such an immediate and nearly overwhelming longing as he had in that brief moment when he held Elizabeth in his arms.

Perhaps it would be best if they were not to remain here together and alone in this cottage. He turned her bonnet in his hands.

"The rain is too heavy," he muttered. "It would not be safe to leave."

But neither was staying here with her. His father was ill. It was likely that Darcy would soon come into his inheritance. He had a sister, a much younger sister, who would need him, and there were tenants and lands and staff who would be relying on him to be focused and able.

Just at that moment, nature punctuated his thoughts with a deep grumbling roll of thunder. Whether Elizabeth liked it or not and whether he found it safe or not to remain here with her, leaving was presently an ill-advised proposition. They would just have to make the best of it unless...

He turned toward the door and considered the option carefully before turning back to her. "I will leave. I will make sure the fire is enough to keep you warm and chase away the damp. We will have a cup of tea, and then I shall leave."

Her look of shocked displeasure from a moment ago when he had kept her from recovering her hat slid into one of confusion. "But this is your cottage, sir. If anyone should leave, it should be me. I am the interloper. There is no need for you to suffer the discomfort of the weather."

"No," he said when she took a slight pause. "What sort of gentleman would I be if I allowed a lady to wander out into the storm, facing the ravages of the weather and the perils of an unfamiliar countryside? It is insupportable. You must remain here, and I will shelter with my horse. Then, when the rain has eased, I shall make my way home. I know this country far better than you. Even with a layer of fog as thick as porridge, I will be able to pick my way home unscathed."

"But you will catch a chill!"

"And you would not?"

She folded her arms, a gesture at which she seemed to be quite proficient.

"I would not be sitting in the damp air for who knows how long before beginning my journey," she retorted

He rounded the table and made his way towards her. "No," he said, "you would be soaked through in minutes and wandering the hillside. That would be so much better." He held her bonnet out to her. "This will not even keep one hair dry. If I allow you to leave this cottage, I will be party to your demise, and that is something I refuse to be."

She took her bonnet from him and lifting her chin, said nothing. Instead, she returned to her seat near the fire, placed her hat on her lap, and began repairing her hair.

Darcy stalked to the fire and gave it a stir before adding a small log. "If you are thinking of not heeding my words and escaping before the tea is ready, you must know that I will follow you, and then we both will be in danger of catching a chill or worse."

She glared at him, and an uneasy silence crept

over the room as the fire snapped and crackled its way to life.

Darcy rose from nursing the fire and retrieved a kettle of water. It was the same kettle that his father always used upon first arriving at the cottage, and it was the kettle that Darcy would see filled with water before leaving, just as his father had always done and instructed him to do. There was nothing better than finding solitude in front of a fire with a cup of tea. That is what his father had always said and what Darcy had come to know as truth. However, today his solitude would not be as it normally was. Today, he would not sit silently before the hearth and watch the flames as he contemplated his future and that of his estate.

He stared at the kettle where it hung over the flames. His estate... He glanced at the beguiling and palpably displeased Elizabeth Bennet, who was nearly finished repairing her hair and looking very much as if she was preparing for a journey, and shook his head. She was stubborn!

"How often do you visit your aunt?" If he could engage her in some conversation, she might not flee from safety. He had an aunt who was stubborn to a fault and would not hesitate to jump headlong into some untenable situation just because she had determined to do so and could not be moved. Elizabeth seemed more intelligent than that. Therefore, he would attempt to sway her from her resolve.

She arched a brow at him, skepticism etched in her features as if she knew his plan.

"Not so often as I would like."

"And how often would you wish to visit your aunt?" Darcy asked as he settled into a chair next to her.

She drew a breath and released it slowly while staring into the fire as her fingers toyed with the ribbon on her bonnet. The right corner of her mouth tipped up while a soft expression settled into her eyes. "Daily." The word was spoken softly and followed by a small sigh. "But that is not possible." She turned her eyes toward him and her lips curved into an unsatisfied smile. "Therefore, I shall have to satisfy myself with once every three years." Her eyes returned to their observation of the fire. "The distance and cost are too great for it to happen more often."

"That is unfortunate."

"Indeed, it is." Her shoulders lifted and lowered

in a shallow shrug. "However, when one has a mother with a love of shopping and four sisters who require care and clothing the same as she does, frequent trips for pleasure with no hope of marriage as the happy result of such an expenditure is simply insupportable."

There was a hint of bitterness to her tone.

"Do you travel alone?"

She shook her head. "My aunt and uncle, as well as my eldest sister, travel with me. Mrs. Foley is my aunt's aunt, though she is more of a mother than an aunt."

"Your other sisters and your mother do not travel with you?"

Again, Elizabeth shook her head, but this time added a small laugh. "Unless there is a favourable chance of finding either a plethora of shops or single gentlemen, my mother is not inclined to undertake a journey nor are my two youngest sisters, although they are far from marriageable age."

"And what of your other sister? You did say you had four sisters, did you not?"

Elizabeth nodded.

"So far, you have only mentioned three."

"You cipher well," she replied with a teasing smile.

Darcy's lips tipped up into a happy expression of their own accord. Teasing was not always something he endured with any significant amount of pleasure. However, when the source of such teasing was as pretty as the lady beside him and filled with the good humour so evident in her expression, it became not something to be endured, but rather something to be sought and entered into with abandon.

"My tutor would be pleased to hear that. I confess learning the facts and figures was not difficult, but it was never so interesting as what might be happening outside the window. Therefore, it took me longer to learn them than it should have and tried the patience of both my tutor and my father. Fortunately, the reprimands I received were not excessively harsh."

The enchanting sparkle of amusement in her eyes caused him to cease speaking. She was captivating. Simply captivating. How he would force himself to go sit with his horse instead of here by her side was beyond him. He pushed up from his seat and crossed to the fire to retrieve the kettle and begin preparing the tea.

"I must say such a confession surprises me," Elizabeth said. "You strike me as a very determined and focused sort of individual, not the sort who would stare out windows when work must be done."

He glanced at her but then returned his eyes to watching the water pour from the kettle into the teapot. "I am. Now. Most times. However, it is a learned skill, based, I suppose, on a natural inclination. But about your fourth sister. Why does she not travel with you?"

He smiled at the teapot after a quick glance in her direction had informed him that her hat was no longer on her lap but resting near the leg of her chair. For now, it seemed, she was content to remain where she was and converse with him rather than fleeing into the gathering storm.

A deep growl of thunder rumbled through the cottage.

"The onslaught grows near," he said as he covered the tea and return to his chair while it steeped.

Elizabeth looked up at the ceiling. "It sounds as if it is nearly overhead."

Darcy nodded. "I would imagine it nearly is. Your fourth sister, the one who is next in age to you?" He prompted.

"Mary would be pleased to have been allowed to join Jane and me on our journey. However, Mama insisted that two young ladies for whom to care were enough trouble for her brother and his wife, seeing as there was also their baby to consider and the fact that my aunt is increasing and quite tired because of it. It mattered not to my mother that three sets of helping hands and watching eyes would allow our aunt more rest. The carriage would be more cramped, and according to Mama, confined spaces, cramped conditions, and a lack of freedom to fidget and move would be excessively unpleasant for one who is in the early stages of increasing." Elizabeth shrugged. "For Mama, that is most likely true, but as Aunt Gardiner says, 'each lady is an individual.' However, our mother could not be moved, and our father thought it best to keep Mary at home."

She turned towards him, and the twinkling in her eyes caught him by surprise. He would have expected such a recital of facts to be accompanied by a look of exasperation or censure, not amusement.

Leaning towards him, she lowered her voice and said, "I suspect Papa insisted on Mary remaining home so that he would have someone capable of sensible conversation to visit with him in his book room."

Darcy's brows furrowed. "Your mother and youngest sisters are incapable of sensible conversation?"

"Sadly, yes."

It seemed odd to Darcy that Elizabeth would have such a mother. Most of the mothers and daughters he had met whether in town or in the country were very much like each other. Therefore, if a mother was insensible, her daughter was likely to be the same. Yet Elizabeth was far from insensible.

"Is it because they are truly incapable or because they choose to be incapable?" Darcy asked.

Elizabeth's lips turned downward as her eyebrows drew together while she considered his question.

"I had never contemplated the cause," she said.

He had suspected as much from her confused expression.

"Mama seems to lack any great ability to be sensible for extended periods of time, and I do not believe it to be an act. Lydia and Kitty are much like Mama."

"But being young, might they not be taught?" Darcy asked.

The look of confusion remained on Elizabeth's face but her left brow arched. "It is entirely possible, I suppose."

Chapter 3

Darcy rose to fetch the tea. "I eventually learned my figures and how to focus on the task at hand rather than the view outside the window. It is, in my opinion, absolutely possible for a young man or lady to learn how to alter their natural tendencies if there is an aptitude for learning."

"Neither of my youngest sisters is without the ability to learn. Having the desire to learn is something completely different."

The teapot chattered against the rim of the cup. Elizabeth was standing at his side, and her presence was causing him some unease. It was not an unpleasant unease. It was once again his desires which plagued him. How the lady's mere presence at his side could cause such a reaction befuddled him. He usually held himself in good regulation without much effort. But not today. Not here. Not with her.

"I fear I have no cream or sugar to offer." He lifted the cup and saucer from the counter, turned toward her, and extended them in invitation.

"I'm sure I shan't miss them." As she took the tea from him, her hand grazed his in the lightest, smallest touch.

While it might have only been a fleeting glance of contact between them, it was enough for him to need to wait until she had returned to her seat before he thought himself capable of lifting his own tea without sloshing it over the rim. Good heavens, she was unsettling! No matter how much he desired to linger over this cup of tea while conversing with her, he knew that he needed to make his escape soon while he still held some resolve to do so.

As if the weather was attempting to mirror his state of mind, the shutters rattled as the wind grew in its intensity, a clap of thunder driving it forward. Darcy lifted his cup and took a sip of its contents before saying, "I am very glad to not be out in it."

Elizabeth smiled at him sheepishly. "As am I." She placed her tea and saucer on the table that stood between them. "I find I must thank you for your insistence that I remain, and I feel almost as if I should apologize for causing you to have to behave in such a high-handed fashion in order to see me safe."

Her smile turned impertinent and, with shaking hands, Darcy relinquished his tea to the table but not without first spilling a portion of it on his waistcoat.

"Blast," he muttered, brushing at the wetness with the palm of his hand. "I assure you I am usually not so clumsy."

It was her infernal ability to rattle him with the slightest enchanting expression that had a most disconcerting effect on him. He glanced up at her.

Her lips were concealed behind her hand, but he could tell from her eyes that she was thoroughly amused by his predicament. At least, he consoled himself, she seemed unaware that she was the cause of his lack of grace

"If you remove it and hang it in front of the hearth, the heat from the fire will have it dried much more quickly than your hand will." The comment was followed by a small laugh – a small, charming laugh – that she was unable to catch and that caused him to smile.

"Forgive me," she continued, "I had not meant to startle you with my confession." She covered her lips with her fingers while her eyes continued to dance with merriment.

Darcy began to unbutton his waistcoat. "You will not be shocked and appalled if I am missing an article of clothing from my ensemble?" His lips twitched. Her good humour was contagious.

She leaned back in her chair, picked up her cup, and replied, "I shall be perfectly at ease."

And she did look it, sitting in such a relaxed fashion and smiling behind her cup as she sipped her tea. How he would love to see her sitting just so and teasing him every day! He turned away from her while he shrugged out of his coat and began removing his waistcoat as he argued against his attraction to her.

She was young, perhaps too young for him to be considering in such a fashion. He shook his head slightly. His father was nqt long for this earth, and Pemberley was a large estate. While Elizabeth appeared to be the age of many who married during their first season and she possessed the intelligence — and even likely some of the training necessary — to run an estate, he was uncertain if asking her to consider taking on the monumental task of the care of him and his home just so he could have his desires assuaged was something about which he should even be thinking.

He placed a chair with a straight ladderback in front of the fire and draped his waistcoat over it. As he was turning to make some comment to Elizabeth about it drying quickly, the door opened and a person he knew well stepped into the cottage.

"What brings you here?" Darcy asked.

Of all the people to arrive unannounced anywhere, George Wickham was the least welcome in Darcy's opinion. The conniving scoundrel was often the source of one scandal or another, although he was ordinarily sly enough for his name not to be associated with said scandal. On the odd occasion when Wickham's name did become attached to a scandal, Darcy was the one left scrambling to repair whatever damage had been done because Darcy loved his father, and his father doted on his godson. So, while Darcy disapproved of Wickham's actions in the most robust sense of the word, he felt compelled to hide Wickham's dissipation from his father as Darcy would not be the source of heartache for a parent he loved so well.

"What? No word of greeting?" Wickham taunted as he shook rain from his hat.

Wickham's flippant, sneering attitude always drove Darcy to distraction. It was as if the man was unable to consider life seriously or to realize that by behaving as he did – throwing money away on cards, chasing every pretty girl he met, and dallying with those with fewer scruples or weaker minds – had any long-lasting consequences. Darcy continued to hold out hope that eventually, as he aged, Wickham would mature and take hold of the good principles which Darcy knew both his own father and Wickham's father had attempted to instill within George. However, with each passing season, that hope increasingly faded as Wickham appeared to grow more and more set in his dissipated ways.

"Well, isn't this a cozy scene?" As he removed his greatcoat, Wickham's eyes had come to rest on Elizabeth. "I dare say if your father knew you had such handsome company, he'd not have sent me to ensure you are well."

Wickham's eyes raked Elizabeth's form, and Darcy stepped between them.

"Miss Bennet is simply taking shelter until the rain has passed." Darcy attempted to keep his tone calm and flat. However, the way Wickham's lips curled into a mocking smile made it nearly impossible, and he was certain a small bit of his anger at Wickham's implication that Miss Bennet was anything but virtuous slipped into his words.

"And that is why you are disrobing?" Wickham laughed.

Darcy snatched up his jacket from his chair and began putting it on. "I spilled tea on my waistcoat. I simply removed it and placed it in front of the fire so it could dry." He tipped his head toward the kitchen. "There is still tea in the pot if you would like a cup, and room before the fire for your things to dry."

Wickham nodded his acceptance but before moving to place his things before the fire or retrieve a cup of tea, he bowed and extended his pleasure in meeting Elizabeth. "How came you to be in need of shelter?" he asked as he draped his coat across the second straight-backed chair Darcy had brought from the table to the hearth.

"I was walking, and when the sky grew dark, and since a tree dared to try to snatch my bonnet from my head, I thought to seek shelter. Fortunately, I remembered seeing this cottage on a previous walk and was able to find it before the rain began."

The way Elizabeth had pulled herself straight and held her cup primly did not go unnoticed by Darcy. There was a wariness about her now that even when he had startled her by his arrival had not existed. Was it his terse greeting of Wickham or Wickham's vulgar implication of what was happening between her and Darcy that caused it, or did she innately suspect that the man was not to be trusted? Darcy would have loved to have asked her, but, unfortunately, that was not possible. So, for now, he would remain curious and be glad that no matter the reason, she did not seem at ease with Wickham.

"You are fortunate," Wickham said as he brought his tea from the kitchen to where they sat near the hearth. The room was one of considerable size, featuring a small kitchen in one corner and a table at the other end and to the right of the door with a large hearth between the kitchen and table.

"I would indeed say I am," Elizabeth replied. "I was able to find this place before one drop of rain fell."

Wickham chuckled. "While that is fortunate indeed, it is not what I meant."

Elizabeth's brow furrowed. "It is not?"

Wickham shook his head and looked at Darcy. "My friend is not known for welcoming strangers. I'm truly shocked he allowed you entrance."

"I have found Mr. Darcy to be nothing but welcoming – a trifle high-handed in compelling me to stay, but in all, a perfect gentleman. Are you certain you have known him long?" Elizabeth asked.

Darcy, who wanted to leap into the conversation and defend himself, remained silent. He had seen the way Elizabeth's left brow had arched when Wickham described him as *my friend*. He was confident that such a look, coupled with her wariness, indicated that she did not believe Wickham and was about to discover the truth. In his mind, it would be far better for her to discover

Wickham's less charming side on her own than through his own defence of himself.

"I have known him all my life." Wickham relaxed back into his chair and casually crossed his ankles in front of him.

He was perfectly at ease, just as he always seemed to be. There was not much which seemed to ruffle Wickham's charming feathers. It was this carefree manner which Darcy had seen Wickham use to win over people, both young and old, servant and superior, worldly wise and innocently naïve. It was perhaps his most dangerous ability, for, with this ease, he seemed able to convince many that he was all he pretended to be. However, Darcy had seen behind the façade because Wickham had one major weakness – jealousy. He wanted what Darcy had, and he did not seem to care if Darcy knew it.

"My father and Darcy's father are friends from childhood. While Darcy's father was born to wealth and position, my own father was not. He is but a solicitor who has become a part of his friend's staff."

"How lovely," Elizabeth inserted before Wickham could continue.

"Lovely?" As that unrestrained question flew from Wickham's mouth, Darcy saw Wickham's composure falter for the briefest of moments.

"Oh, indeed!" Elizabeth exclaimed. "To be so connected to a lifelong friend must be simply wonderful. My uncle Philips is a solicitor, and he finds great pleasure in being able to provide his friends with the service they need. I do not believe he would be happy doing anything else. It is as if he were born to the position, which he was not. He fell into it rather by chance." As she spoke, Elizabeth tilted her head and studied Wickham. "My uncle hopes one day to pass on his business to his son just as my grandfather passed it on to him. Will you be following your father's footsteps?"

Chapter 4

Darcy fought to contain his amusement at Wickham's apparent inability to formulate a quick response. More than her beauty, Elizabeth's keen mind and this particular ability to leave a man speechless who was known for possessing a silver tongue recommended her to Darcy as the best possible choice for his future wife. When the storm passed, he would see her home and then invite her to visit him and Pemberley so that she could meet both his father and his sister.

Feeling the happiness that such thoughts brought him, he entered the conversation. "Our fathers would prefer for him to take orders since there is a valuable living within my father's power to bestow."

"A member of the clergy?" Elizabeth looked genuinely shocked at the suggestion, which caused

Darcy's lips to twitch with barely contained amusement.

"It is a respectable and worthwhile profession," she continued, "and I know I have only just met you, Mr. Wickham, and am being entirely too forward by half, but I must say I question the wisdom in such a thing."

"How so?" Darcy attempted to make the question sound excessively serious while within he was delighted to hear Elizabeth suggest that Wickham would not make a good man of the cloth.

"Yes, yes," Wickham said, finally finding his tongue. "I should also like to know your reasoning as I think I should be good at giving sermons."

"But would you enjoy it?" Elizabeth asked.

"I do not see why I would not. The living is substantial, and the duties are not excessive. In fact, the living includes a rector who would provide me with all the assistance I should need, so that the office would never become burdensome."

Darcy watched Elizabeth pull her bottom lip between her teeth, furrow her brow, relax it, arched her left eyebrow, and tip her head. Eagerly, he waited to hear her thoughts.

"I do not doubt, sir," Elizabeth began after a

moment of silent contemplation, "that you possess the ability to deliver a sermon in a most enjoyable fashion. You appear to me to be always at ease, and I would venture a guess that you are a natural conversation partner with the ability to discuss a wide range of topics with relatively little effort."

The accuracy of Elizabeth's musing astounded Darcy.

"Such a talent," she continued, "lends itself well to becoming a parson or a solicitor. However," she paused, and Darcy imagined, from the way her eyes narrowed slightly and her lips pursed, that she was selecting her next words carefully. "Only moments ago, you admitted that you and Mr. Darcy have known each other all your life. Yet, you seem to not truly understand who he is. Added to that, you made accusations about me without ever having met me. While a solicitor might find such flaws in character to be of little hindrance in his work, the same cannot be said for a parson. The man tasked with the responsibility to care for his parish and its needs would find such an inability to understand the people around and closest to him — as well as the propensity to assume the worst without gathering the facts — to be a great detriment to completing his duties with any great degree of effectiveness."

Rising, Darcy gathered both his and Elizabeth's empty cup. He needed to have something to do with his hands rather than applauding Elizabeth's speech, which appeared to have had a very unsettling effect on Wickham. Darcy crossed to the kitchen and placed the dishes on the workbench just as Wickham began to respond.

"That is a very pretty speech." His voice carried less of his usual charm than it had moments ago.

Yes, thought Darcy, Wickham was most decidedly affronted.

"In fact," Wickham continued, "I daresay it is nearly pretty enough to capture Darcy's attention and potentially his fortune." Wickham relaxed further into his chair, placed his cup beside him on the table, and, propping his elbows on the arms of his chair, steepled his fingers. "The ladies in town should try such a tactic, for none of them have yet succeeded in snaring the great Fitzwilliam Darcy, although many have tried." One shoulder lifted and lowered in a half shrug. "But then, none, not even you, have a hope of claiming his fortune other than the gifts he might bestow on her for certain favours, for he is already promised to another. Tell me, Miss Elizabeth, will you be satisfied to simply be his mistress instead of the mistress of Pemberley? For if not, I would suggest you save your fanciful reasonings to impress some other wealthy chap."

Neither the rattling of the shutters by the howling wind nor the rumbling of distant thunder could compare to the fury that flashed in Elizabeth's eyes. Darcy, who had moved toward Wickham ready to do the man harm, stopped dead in his tracks. There was no way he was going to stand between Wickham and what he justly deserved. Darcy would wait his turn and thrash whatever pieces remained when Elizabeth was through.

Elizabeth's hands smoothed the fabric of her dress over her knees as her shoulders rose and fell in time with several deliberate breaths. Then, she folded her hands, lifted her chin, and began to speak.

"Mr. Wickham, were this my house, I would gladly have you removed no matter how the storm raged outside. Happily for you, this is not my house. However, I should wonder if Mr. Darcy does not see you on your way soon, for you have not only maligned him, but you have also spoken ill of his guest."

Her hands once again smoothed her skirt as she attempted to calm herself. Darcy could see the battle for regulation play out in the set of her jaw and the twitch of her lips as well as in the narrowing of her enchanting eyes.

"I cannot give a moment's credence to any of the shade you attempt to throw on your friend. For you see, my great aunt has only ever spoken highly of both Mr. Darcy and his father. She is no swift judge of character. Her opinions are based on long and thorough consideration. She would never be so bold as you and throw disparagement on the character of someone she had only just met as you have done to me. I will assure you, Mr. Wickham, that my character is not as you have supposed. I am and always have been circumspect in my behavior. I do not give favours to any gentleman regardless of whether or not he offers gifts, and I assure you that my virtue is intact and will remain so until the day I decide to marry and stand before the vicar to take my vows."

She rose from her chair and moved to stand

behind it. Her fingertips pressed into the cushion on the back as she grasped it firmly.

"I had no intention of attempting to sway Mr. Darcy toward marriage with either my words or actions when I entered this cottage, nor do I have any now. Indeed, I was set to leave this cottage as soon as Mr. Darcy entered, so that such a thing would not happen. What am I to him? A stranger. The niece of a tenant. Naught else. It was his kind heart which compelled me to stay when I would have left." She laughed a small bitter laugh and shook her head. "It was that same kindness that offered you a cup of tea and a place at the fire after you entered and spoke so meanly of both him and me. And it is that kindness that keeps him now from hurling you out into the storm, so that I might have my say."

Darcy nodded and returned the small smile she gave him.

"How you cannot know Mr. Darcy's character after so many years of acquaintance leaves me to wonder if you are either stupid or," her lips pursed and her eyes sparkled, "merely jealous." She shrugged. "And why would you not be? Mr. Darcy is twice the man you could ever hope to be. He is far more handsome. His manners are perfectly refined, and, shall we not overlook the obvious? He has a fortune."

She released her grip on the back of the chair. "But his greatest wealth is not found in his riches, Mr. Wickham. It is found in his noble and honorable character. And those are not things to which one must be born." She smiled at Darcy again. "I should be honored to count him as a friend. And I will add that whoever this lady is to whom he is betrothed is a very fortunate lady indeed, for she will find herself well-cared-for and respected." She shifted her eyes back to Wickham. "Again, those are riches that any man can offer a lady. There is no need to be born to such."

"I am not betrothed," Darcy said.

"You are not?" Elizabeth asked in feigned surprise, causing Darcy to grin. "Do you mean to tell me that none of what Mr. Wickham has said is true?"

"Not a word," Darcy replied. Then, he tipped his head. "No, I am incorrect. He is the son of my father's friend and solicitor. That much is true." He held up a finger. "And I am not always welcoming to strangers. I find it trying to meet new people."

"Well, that is a fault to be sure," Elizabeth replied lightly. "But then, some of us new people can be rather trying."

Darcy chuckled and then turned to Wickham. "I believe Miss Elizabeth is correct. It is time that you left. Your disparagement of myself, while I do not condone it, I can bear. However, I cannot and will not forebear such treatment of any guest in my home – most especially not of Miss Elizabeth. The thunder grows distant. The worst is over. Please inform my father that I will return after I have seen Miss Elizabeth safely returned to her aunt."

Wickham sneered but rose from his chair. "And what do you think he will say when I tell him how I found you? Indeed, what will everyone say when they hear the tale I have to tell?" He looked past Darcy to Elizabeth. "You did not think you could lecture me as you did without paying some price now did you?"

"If they believe you, then they are greater fools than you," Elizabeth returned.

"Fools they may be, but ruined you will be," Wickham retorted.

And with those words, Darcy found the end of his patience while his fist found Wickham's jaw.

Wickham yelped in pain, his right hand flying to rub his jaw, as he scooted away from Darcy.

"You will say nothing to besmirch Miss Elizabeth," Darcy growled, "or I will call you out."

"And what of your father? He will be greatly displeased with you for it. I am his favourite."

"Get out," Darcy shouted. "I will no longer hide your indiscretions from him. See how long his preference lasts when he learns of all you have done."

"One word," Wickham spat back, "and I will tell how you were here with her." His chin jutted in the direction of Elizabeth.

"Out!" Darcy moved to extract the scoundrel bodily if necessary, but being the coward Wickham was, he quickly snatched his things and reached the door before Darcy had the pleasure of laying a hand on him.

As the loud rattling of an angrily closed door rang through the cottage, Darcy threw the latch and turned towards Elizabeth. "He will not be allowed entrance," Darcy assured her. "And I will not be leaving until we leave together. I have not one morsel of trust in him. I have seen and heard about far too much reprehensible behaviour where he is concerned."

Darcy moved quickly across the room as he spoke to where Elizabeth stood with her arms wrapped around herself. "Are you well?"

Elizabeth nodded and gave him a wavering smile. "I am until he tells his tale. Then, I am ruined, and my whole family tainted." She shook her head as she looked toward the ceiling. "I should never have stayed."

Darcy placed a hand on each of her upper arms and drew her close. "You stayed because you are wise," he said as he wrapped her in his embrace. She was trembling, so he rubbed her back reassuringly. "You will not suffer because of him.

She pushed away from him but only just. She did not move so far that his arms could not still encircle her.

"How can I not? You said yourself that he is not to be trusted. He is angry with me, he dislikes you, and therefore, he has no reason not to whisper about this into the ear of anyone willing to listen. My aunt," she paused and pressed her lips together to keep them from trembling, "and my sister, they will be so disappointed." A tear slid down her cheek.

"We shall tell the tale before he does, and I doubt he realizes who your aunt is." He brushed the tear from her cheek. "I dare say there is not a soul in all of Derbyshire who would dare to believe one ill word about her great niece." He smiled down at her. "Mrs. Foley is well respected, as is her brother, and there are very few who would dare to speak against the vicar of Kympton."

"Are you certain?"

Darcy nodded and released her from his embrace. "I am. Did you mean what you said about the lady who marries me being fortunate?"

Her brow furrowed as her lashes fluttered over confused eyes. "I did."

"Then," Darcy paused to wipe his suddenly moist hands on his breeches. He swallowed and willed his heart not to race so fast that it would explode. "Would you consider being that lady?"

Her mouth dropped open as shock suffused her face. She shook her head. "We have only just met. We are little more than strangers. I was not being anything less than honest when I said I did not intend to persuade you into marrying me. I know

I am a gentleman's daughter, and you are a gentleman's son and as such we are not unequal. However, Longbourn could be contained within Pemberley many times over. The spheres in which we move are so very different."

"I do not ask you to gain position or wealth." He moved a fraction of an inch closer to her. It was not that there was a significant gap between where he stood and where she was, but her words made him feel as if a great chasm was about to appear in front of them, dashing all the fledgling hope that had formed in his heart since finding her here in his cottage.

"I do not even ask because I fear any scandal will arise from our sojourn here. I ask because my heart demands it." He shook his head and shrugged. "I do not understand this need. I only know that I feel as if I have found a dear friend whom I shall grieve most severely if she is not at my side." He smiled and laughed lightly. "Your aunt's brother has always said 'do not seek a wife; seek a companion for your future life.' I never understood him until now." He shrugged. "I always thought he was attempting to make the selection of the mistress for my estate and the mother of its heir into something of a pious platitude. But he was not. I see that now in your eyes. I hear it in your words, and I feel it in your presence."

"We are little more than strangers," Elizabeth repeated.

"Allow me to borrow a story from the vicar's arsenal and ask you how long Isaac knew Rebekah before he loved her?"

"That is not the same," she said shaking her head. "Our society is not their society."

"But cannot the same God who worked in the lives of the ancients also work in our present day?"

Her eyes narrowed, and her lips pursed as she folded her arms and shook her head. "You are being impossible. We do not know enough about each other to tie ourselves together for life."

There was a slight curve to the side of her mouth that gave him to know that she was not as set against him as she might try to appear to be.

"I am not proposing we marry this instant. I only wish to know if you would allow me to call on you with the intention that one day – when you have discovered that I am right and that we are well-suited to one another – we will marry."

"When I discover that you are right?" She said with a laugh. "You, sir, are very determined."

"Never more so," he replied with a grin. Indeed, he had never in all of his life felt as certain about anything as he did about the fact that he knew he was having just one of the many arguments he would have with his future wife. Wife. It was a word that normally made him quake. But not now. Not here. Not with her.

He scooted around her and snatched up her bonnet from where it still lay beside the leg of her chair.

"My hat!" she cried.

"And a very pretty one it is."

"You are not seriously planning to hold my hat ransom until I agree to consider becoming your wife, are you?"

Darcy shrugged and turned her bonnet in his hand before hiding it behind his back. "It worked to keep you from venturing out into the storm, and if it worked once..." He shrugged again.

She shook her head. "I cannot deny that I would very much like to learn more about you, nor can I say that your proposal does not intrigue me.

However, you must know that I will not be easily persuaded."

"Then, you will accept my offer of a possible future marriage?"

She nodded. "Now might I have my bonnet?"

He shook his head even as he drew the bonnet out from behind his back and stepped towards her. "Not until we have sealed our agreement with a kiss," he said as he placed her bonnet on her head before tipping her chin and looking down into her eyes. "May I?"

"But we are not betrothed."

"Oh, but we are."

"You are an impossible man!"

"Indeed, but may I kiss you?"

She drew a breath and released it as her eyes lowered for a moment before returning to his. "You may, but..."

He did not wait for her conditions but bent and claimed her lips. As he wrapped his arms around her and pulled her close, relishing in the softness of her form, his body groaned, warning him of the storm he would have to face in controlling his desires, and thunder rumbled in the distance as if it was taking its leave, having completed its work in bringing these two together.

Morning Mist

Wonderful enchantment can be found in the early mist of morning

Chapter 1

As she climbed the hill near her new home, Barton Cottage, Marianne Dashwood hummed the tune of the new piece of music she was currently learning while her fingers occasionally moved along an imaginary set of keys.

She and her sisters and mother had only been at Barton Cottage a short time, and it was nothing like Norland, the estate on which Marianne had grown up. However, it did have some enchantments. Some of those enchantments were these hills and the meadow just at the top of this particular one — especially at this time of day when the morning's mist was just rising to make way for the day ahead.

As she reached the top of the mound, she paused both her walking and humming, lifted her face to the sun, and pulled in a deep breath of fresh morning air – air that had yet to be used by many since most people would likely still be lying in bed or preparing for the day.

There were servants, of course, who had been up since before the first tantalizing fingers of sunshine had begun to stir and part the mist which hung over the hills and valleys surrounding Barton Cottage. However, there would be few servants wandering the fields as she was. They would be busy baking bread, tending children, seeing to the animals, and other such tasks as were expected of them. Theirs was a life of hard work, and the thought of such caused Marianne to sigh. How dreadful it must be to live such a life where greeting the morning with exuberance would be impossible.

At the melancholy thought of missing the delights of these hills and meadows, an idea sprang to Marianne's mind. She would gather some flowers and place them around the cottage. Surely, that would give Walter and Mary a small portion of the wonder and beauty she experienced on these morning rambles.

She was confident that there was nothing more refreshing in the entire world than a walk in the morning mist. Here, the visions she gathered from the stories and poems she read, as well as the songs she played, could run free — galloping up the hills, descending down the valleys, rising on wings into the air.

A walk in the countryside at any time of day was delicious. However, in these early hours of the morning, when the dew still clung to the grass and flowers and when the clouds, which had descended to touch the ground, bringing with them the dreams found upon one's bed, were beginning to rise and depart, a walk was more than delicious. It was magical. She almost expected to meet some gallant knight returning to his castle after successfully vanquishing his foe.

She rubbed her hands up and down her arms. The air was cool, but the day had appeared too lovely to wear her brown pelisse. Brown could be such a dull colour, and today was not a dull day! And so, she had ventured out with only her shawl to ward off the mischievous little pixies who delighted in causing a lady's skin to bump and her muscles to shiver. Marianne could not help but smile at the idea of pixies being shooed away by the motion of her hands as she warmed her skin.

The sound of a falcon's cry and the snort of a horse drew her from her reverie and urged her to discover their source. With any luck, it would be *him*.

She had come upon him – an intriguing stranger — yesterday morning, and she had watched him from a distance, advancing and retreating, parrying, and lunging as he fought an imaginary foe. She had been mesmerized with the movement of his feet and the form of his arms. She imagined he was likely an excellent dancer since his steps were light, quick, and precise. His carriage was erect and noble, and his arms strong and steady.

She had been transfixed where she stood, completely and utterly incapable of alerting him to her presence. And so, she had watched until he had sheathed his sword and turned to leave. Then, she had hurried away, fearful that he might discover she had been watching him.

It was not polite for a young lady to stand and stare at anyone. Her sister Eleanor had reminded Marianne of that many times throughout her life. But how could one, as curious as she, refrain from occasionally watching something of interest, especially when that something was actually someone very reminiscent of a knight from days of old?

Quietly, so as not to draw notice to herself, she took up the same vantage point as yesterday, near a tree at the edge of the meadow. A skittering of delight danced up her spine. It was him, and he was dressed exactly as he had been yesterday with boots that shone in the sunlight, breaches which stretched smoothly across muscular thighs, and a shirt of billowy fine white lawn that was open at the neck. He wore no cravat, no waistcoat, no jacket, and no hat. Wisps of his light brown hair moved freely as the wind blew, and his complexion appeared to be browned by the sun as if his hat were a thing he often forewent wearing. He did not appear to be classically handsome, but there was something about him – an aura which proclaimed him to be far more desirable than any classic dandy. In Marianne's opinion, he was simply magnificent.

The falcon soared above him, dipping and circling, and then when the intriguing stranger whistled, the animal came to rest on his outstretched arm. Other than the customary chickens, pheasants, geese, and ducks, Marianne had never seen a bird at such a close distance as he was to his falcon. She had definitely never held any of the fowl that she had seen! The sight of the falcon resting on his arm captured her imagination, and she longed to step out from the shadows of the trees and make her presence known, so that she could see the creature even more closely.

However, she was reluctant to disturb the gentleman before her as he spoke softly to the animal while reaching into the bag which hung at his waist and drawing out some morsel of food which he presented to his bird. Marianne marvelled at how gentle both master and falcon now appeared when just moments ago both had looked wary and prepared to take on some foe even if the enemy proved only to be a pheasant or a mouse.

Marianne attempted to remain perfectly still as she waited and watched while silently hoping he would send the bird flying once again before her position of covert observation was discovered. However, she was not successful, for as she shifted to make herself more comfortable leaning against the tree, the falcon noticed her and alerted his master to her presence with a loud cry and a slight flapping of his wings.

"Good morning," the stranger said, turning towards her.

Marianne pushed off the tree where she was leaning, stepped forward two paces, and extended a greeting of her own. "I did not wish to disturb you or frighten your falcon," she explained. It was not a complete falsehood. She had not wished to disturb them. She also had not wished to be discovered, but that part did not need to be said. "Is it safe for me to approach?"

"Yes, Lorcan is relatively gentle," he replied. "He is no lapdog, but he has been flying for Sir John and myself for several years."

Marianne approached slowly for, though the stranger said the bird was gentle, it was still a bird of prey with sharp talons and only a partially tamed heart. "This is Sir John's bird?"

The eyes of the handsome gentleman before her lit with humour. "It was an entirely self-serving gift from me to him three years ago. I tired of only hunting with dogs."

"Do you visit Barton Park often then?" She hoped he did, for she would very much like to see him there. Sir John could be interesting, but he could also be a bore. And he and his mother-in-law, Mrs. Jennings, enjoyed teasing and gossip far more than Marianne could abide. And then there was Mrs. Sir John, Lady Middleton, who cared for little save her horribly spoiled children. If *he* were at Barton Park, then there would be a delightful reason to suffer the others.

"Indeed, I do. Sir John is a friend of long-standing. And you, do you visit there often?"

"We have only just arrived at Barton Cottage. However, we do dine there as often as Sir John can convince my mother to do so. You must be the colonel whom Sir John was telling us would be visiting." From Sir John's intelligence about his friend, Marianne had expected some old, balding, and somewhat portly fellow. She had not thought that any friend of Sir John's, let alone one who was retired, would be so dignified, yet with a deliciously tantalizing liveliness lying behind his reserved façade. There was more to the gentleman before her than what he presented. She could just feel it.

"Colonel Christopher Brandon at your service," he said with a gallant nod of his head.

Marianne was certain that if he had not been holding a bird on his arm, his bow would have been executed with perfect grace. He just seemed the sort who would be a gentleman through and through.

"And you must be one of the Miss Dashwoods about whom I have heard so much," he continued with a smile as he prepared to send his falcon flying once again. "One more turn of the sky for my friend here, and then he must be returned to his home," he explained.

"I am Marianne, the second eldest Dashwood," Marianne said as she tipped her head back and watched the bird rise into the air with great powerful flaps of his wings. As she shielded the sun from her eyes, Lorcan's wings held their position as he soared.

"He is beautiful," Marianne murmured.

"That he is," Colonel Brandon agreed. "There is something rather special about the mixture of power and grace."

"Oh, indeed!" Marianne cried. She had been thinking the very same words.

"*My heart leaps up when I behold a falcon in the sky,*" he began.

Marianne smiled with delight. She enjoyed poetry nearly as much as she enjoyed music. "It is a rainbow, sir."

"While a rainbow is delightful, I prefer the majesty of a falcon in flight," he answered before continuing the poem:

> So was it when my life began;
>
> So is it now I am a man;
>
> So be it when I shall grow old,
>
> Or let me die!
>
> The Child is father of the Man;
>
> And I could wish my days to be
>
> Bound each to each by natural piety.[1]

A sigh escaped Marianne as she listened to the short poem. Colonel Brandon's voice was the sort that she preferred. It was neither too high nor too low in tone. She would willingly listen to him read or recite all day. There was a musical quality to his voice.

1. *My Heart Leaps Up by William Wordsworth*

"Do you sing?" she asked as the excitement of the prospect of hearing him behind her while she played overtook her.

"I have not in years." He whistled for his bird.

Marianne's hand flew to her heart. "You have not sung in years? How do you manage it?"

He cast a quick glance her direction and chuckled as he once again rewarded Lorcan for returning to his arm. "It was only trying at first," he assured her. "Thomas," he called to a groom who stood with the horse.

Marianne had not noticed there was anyone else with them. But there was Thomas, whom she had seen once when arriving in Sir John's carriage for dinner on one of the occasions when her mother had accepted an invitation. She nodded and murmured a greeting to him, then, waited and watched as a hood was placed on the falcon and the majestic bird was placed in a box to be taken back to his home at Barton Park.

Chapter 2

"May I join you on your walk, Miss Marianne?" the colonel asked.

"Oh, I am not going any further. Mama will be worried if I am gone too long, and then she will send either Elinor or Margaret to find me." It was too bad, really. She would like to spend more time with Colonel Brandon, but she did not want to risk having to share him with one of her sisters.

"Then, may I see you home?" he asked as he put on his jacket and fastened the buttons.

It was a delightful suggestion that drew a pleased smile from Marianne. "That would be lovely, Colonel, but first, I must gather some flowers." Her eyes followed his fingers as he straightened his collar and pulled it closed to be held there by his jacket. It seemed a heavy coat for the warmth of the day.

"I do not mind. In fact, if you require assistance, I am capable of picking flowers and transporting them without damage."

He was teasing. She could see it in his eyes.

"I would not expect you to be incapable. I only worry that it will be too delicate a task for one such as yourself who is used to falcons and such."

Her replying tease found its mark, and he chuckled.

"I assure you that such tasks are not beneath me, though I must shock you once again by admitting to not having gathered flowers for longer than I have foregone singing."

Marianne looked up from where she had stooped to pick some flowers. "No singing and no flowers? I am certain you have been living in misery!"

He shook his head, though unconvincingly. "I would not say misery," was all he said.

She stood and handed him the flower she had just picked. "This one is for you."

She wished to know what he would call it if it was not misery, for both his eyes and his tone had spoken of deep sadness as he said the words. However, she knew that it was not polite to pry into business that did not concern her, though not prying was not easily done. A great deal of fortitude was required for such a thing since she was such a curious creature.

"If I accept this flower, will you be expecting a song in return?"

"Not just yet," she replied before returning to her work of gathering flowers. "Perhaps in a week?"

He chuckled again.

"If there is a song you enjoy and I know it, I would be happy to play while you sang." She looked up from the flowers at him again. She was not certain if she enjoyed admiring his noble features from this aspect or when she was standing better. She supposed it did not matter as long as she was able to admire them. "I could even sing with you if the tune is so familiar that my fingers do not require all my attention."

"I am not even certain I can sing any longer."

Not able to sing! The thought was both shocking and grievous. Surely, anyone who could sing at one time could still sing many years after stopping, could they not?

"The meadow would not tell if you were to attempt the activity and failed." She rose from her place with half a bouquet of flowers. "Nor would I."

His replying smile was slightly sad. "I once knew a lady a lot like you. When I was a young man."

She tipped her head and studied his face. A broken heart could steal the desire to sing or even hear music from anyone, herself included, and she loved music. Therefore, she determined that must be the source of his pain. "Was she pretty?"

Oh, she knew Elinor would scold for asking such a thing, but a tragic tale of love and loss was one of her favourite sorts to read. A small fluttering of trepidation in her stomach told her that hearing a real story of such agony would likely not be so pleasant as reading one.

"She was. Her hair was just a shade darker than yours, and she was your height. Her eyes were a colour very much like the leaf of this flower, and her smile was the most welcoming I have ever seen until today. I had not thought another such smile existed. I am pleased to know I am wrong."

Marianne could feel her cheeks warm at the compliment and had she been alone, she would have buried her nose in the small bouquet she held while allowing herself to smile broadly and revel in the knowledge that he found her smile welcoming. However, she was not alone, so she contained her pleasure in a small smile and said, "She sounds lovely."

He nodded. "She was."

"Did she sing?" Perhaps he no longer sang because doing so reminded him of singing with her.

"No," he replied with a small burst of laughter. "She claimed she would frighten the birds with her croaking, but I dare say she exaggerated. She hummed very well, and she liked listening to me sing to her." He twirled the flower he held. "She also liked flowers."

He had sung to her. Marianne's heart sighed at the wonderfulness of the thought of having a gentleman sing to her. If he were to stop, she would likely always find very little pleasure in music. She placed another flower into her bouquet. "And she is why you no longer sing or gather flowers?"

A great laboured breath was answer enough for Marianne. This girl, whoever she was, had broken the colonel's heart. That fluttering in her stomach had been correct. Hearing a true tale of lost love was not so delightful as reading one. The sorrow it stirred in her was different. It was not created by fanciful images, but rather from the sigh of a wounded man. Such sorrow was the sort that passed from his soul to hers, begging her to find some remedy for it and creating an uneasiness which she knew would last until she had helped him in some way, though she did not know how she could.

He shook his head. "I cannot tell you about it."

"I will not ask," she assured him as she stood from where she was collecting the final flowers needed to make an acceptably cheerful bouquet for the sitting room.

"Time does not heal all wounds," he added.

Marianne's eyes grew wide. "It does not?" She was sure she had never heard such a thing before.

He shook his head again. "It has been years – many years — since we were parted."

Not knowing what to say to such a revelation, Marianne opted instead to place a hand on his arm and smile softly, attempting to convey to him some of the sorrow she felt on his behalf.

"Sir John calls me a silly old fool for not having sought anyone since, and Mrs. Jennings is bent on seeing my sorry, lonely state fixed. Beware of her.

She will have you married off before you know it."
He extended his arm to her. "And she will have
no trouble finding you a suitor, for you are young,
beautiful, and lively. Quite the opposite of me." He
chuckled.

Strangely, it pricked her heart that he would
speak of her finding a suitor.

"Do not fear," she said, "Mrs. Jennings and Sir
John have already been attempting to match my
sisters and me with gentlemen they know. I have
heard little else save how this gentleman or that
one would be a good match." She laughed with
him. "You have even been promoted to my sister
Elinor." Oh, the idea of such a thing as Elinor and
the colonel making a match caused that strange
pricking again, which in turn, caused her to pause
for a moment before continuing, "but having met
you, I can see you would not suit. Elinor is too
grave."

"It is not because I am an old curmudgeon?"

Marianne shook her head. "An old
curmudgeon? I think not! I am certain an old
curmudgeon would not own a falcon." Or look so
dashing while slashing the air with a sword, she
added to herself.

"You are too kind, Miss Marianne. I am ancient compared to you. Twice your age, I would venture."

"Are you thirty-four?"

"Not quite, but in three month's time I will be."

"And I will be eighteen by then, so you will still not be twice my age."

Why it seemed necessary to dissuade the colonel of the belief that he was too old to be considered by one such as she was baffling and astounding. She had always imagined that a gentleman of more than thirty could in no way be appealing, but she had to admit she was as wrong as she was astounded.

"Why there are far older men who are curmudgeons in every sense of the word who are married to ladies not much older than I." She shook her head. "It is not your age that prevents me from promoting my sister to you. It is simply that she is far too grave. She is more of a curmudgeon at nineteen than you will likely ever be." She looked up at him with wide eyes. "Do not tell her I said that. I should hate to cause her pain or bear yet another one of her lectures."

"I shall not say a word. I am flattered that you

do not find me too old. But, I warn you that very like many old curmudgeons, I have a bit of a pain in one leg that afflicts me when the weather is unpleasant."

"Indeed? Is there a cause?"

He shrugged. "It is likely due to a wound I received."

"A wound!" she cried. "Then it is perfectly forgivable."

"It was only a small skirmish," he hastened to add, seemingly uncomfortable that she should exclaim over his injury. "I assure you it was nothing heroic. However, during that fight, I was forcefully removed from my horse, and the lower portion of my leg broke. It has hurt on occasion ever since, but I find it has grown worse in recent years."

They had reached the gate in front of Barton Cottage.

"You are still not an old curmudgeon," Marianne protested. "Will you come in?" While she still had no desire to share his attention with either of her sisters or her mother, she also did not wish for him to leave her.

"It is too early," he replied, "However, I would

not be opposed to calling at some more appropriate time if I am welcome."

"I would like that very much." Her heart actually leapt at the thought of a gentleman as dashing as Colonel Brandon reclining in one of the chairs in their sitting room. "And I am certain my mother will be equally as pleased."

He held the gate open for her. "As will Sir John and Mrs. Jennings, no doubt."

She giggled at the comment even though it strangely pleased her that she would be pleasing Sir John and Mrs. Jennings in such a fashion.

"Will you call today?"

"I cannot today. I am previously engaged. Sir John and I are taking the dogs out for a run."

Disappointment of a larger than expected size settled into her heart. "Tomorrow, then."

He closed the gate, and she turned to go to the house but then turned back. "Will you be in the meadow tomorrow?" She held up her bouquet. "I may need more flowers."

He grinned. "Lorcan will be at home tomorrow, but I intend to visit the meadow."

"Then, perhaps you can help me bring my

flowers home when I have finished collecting them?"

"I would be pleased to be of service to you in such a fashion." He tipped his hat and mounted his horse.

Marianne sighed as she watched him ride away. Today was going to be interminably long.

Chapter 3

"What are you reading, Mama?" Marianne placed her bonnet on the worktable and draped her wrap on the back of one of the chairs that stood at the table.

"Sir John has sent another invitation to dine with him." Mrs. Dashwood sighed and laid the folded missive in her lap. "His generosity is commendable, but this will make three invitations just this week."

Marianne sat down next to her mother with a stack of music to sort through. There had to be one song in this pile which would be familiar to Colonel Brandon. "You will accept, will you not?"

It would make this day far less painfully long if Marianne could be assured of seeing the colonel at Barton Park instead of waiting until tomorrow morning.

"You wish me to accept?" Mrs. Dashwood asked in surprise.

Marianne could not fault her mother's shocked reaction, for had Marianne not met Colonel Brandon, she would have been begging her mother not to force her into company with Sir John and Mrs. Jennings. However, tolerating Sir John and his mother-in-law was a small price to pay in return for a few hours spent with the colonel.

"I do," she answered.

"Who was at the gate with you?" Marianne's younger sister, Margaret, asked as she joined them in the sitting room, followed by their eldest sister, Elinor.

"There was someone at the gate?" Mrs. Dashwood looked at Marianne with a great deal of curiosity.

"His name is Colonel Brandon."

"Sir John's friend?" Elinor asked.

Marianne nodded and continued sorting through the music on her lap. "The very one, but he is not at all as I expected." She pulled a short song from the sheets in her pile. This one would do. He would almost surely know this one.

"And you wish to dine with him so that Mrs.

Jennings might push us together?" Elinor's tone was almost as sharp as the look she gave her sister.

"No!" Marianne said with great feeling. "I have already warned him that you would not suit."

"You did what?" Mrs. Dashwood exclaimed before Elinor could. "A gentleman shows up at our gate, and you tell him that your sister and he will not suit?"

Marianne rose and crossed to her piano. "Oh no. He did not just appear at our gate. I met him in the meadow just over the hill. He was flying his falcon, and I stopped to watch. Have you ever seen such a bird up close, Mother? I assure you it is an awe-inspiring proposition. Their talons are excessively frightening."

"Did you pet the falcon?" Margaret asked.

"I did not dare," Marianne replied. "His name is Lorcan."

"That is a lovely name for a bird," Margaret said.

"It is, is it not?" Marianne agreed. The colonel had exceptional taste — likely in all things. How could he not if he could name a bird so well, like music, and recite poetry?

"About Colonel Brandon," their mother

prompted when Marianne did not continue speaking. "How did he come to be at our gate?"

Marianne lifted her eyes from the sheet of music on her lap. She would have to imagine how the colonel might sound singing this piece later when there were not so many inquisitive people around to interrupt her musings.

"He offered to see me home and was patient enough to wait while I gathered flowers. He really is so much different from what I expected."

"How do you mean?" Elinor asked.

"Is he handsome?" Mrs. Dashwood asked on top of Elinor's question.

"He cannot be." Margaret dropped her pencil on the picture she was sketching at the worktable and looked at her mother in shock. "Sir John said he was thirty-five, and I am certain no one is handsome when they are so old."

"I am older than thirty-five," Mrs. Dashwood said with a pointed look for her youngest daughter. "Are you saying that I am not handsome?"

Margaret laughed. "You are our mother, and therefore, you shall always be handsome to us even when you are quite ancient."

"Whether I am your mother or not, I cannot say

that my looks have been completely spent. I admit my bloom faded some years ago, but I have not faded completely."

"Oh, Mama!" Marianne cried. "You are as handsome as you ever were. Margaret it wrong."

She felt a pang of self-reproof as she declared her sister's thinking to be incorrect, for she herself had assumed as much until this morning. She would have to be less judgmental of such things in the future.

"I am? I think not! Sir John is at least forty, and he is not a whit handsome," Margaret protested.

"I am sure he is handsome enough for Lady Middleton," Elinor chided. "It is not nice to speak so of anyone, least of all Mama's cousin, who has been so gracious to us."

Margaret folded her arms and scowled at Elinor.

Marianne could sympathize with such an expression. Elinor had no sense of passion. To her, one simply did what was right regardless of how one might feel about something.

"Colonel Brandon is handsome," Marianne said. "And he is not thirty-five. He will only be thirty-four on this next birthday."

"Is that why he is not as you imagined?" Elinor asked. "Because he is handsome?"

Marianne nodded. "Partly, yes. I was as mistaken as Margaret until I met Colonel Brandon. There is something rather fascinating about him. He has an excellent build. Tall and strong. His jaw is firm, and his eyes expressive."

"And his hair?" Margaret asked eagerly. "Is it grey?"

"Not a strand! It is perfectly brown," Marianne answered.

"And why would he and Elinor not suit? He sounds like a fine match if he is both handsome and fascinating?" Mrs. Dashwood asked.

"Elinor is too serious. A gentleman such as Colonel Brandon does not need a serious wife. He has enough cares to cause melancholy without a wife to add to it."

"I do not cause melancholy!" Elinor retorted.

"You do sometimes," Margaret mumbled.

"Margaret, that is far too impertinent," Mrs. Dashwood scolded.

"I am only saying that Elinor's personality would not mesh with his," Marianne continued above the ensuing din before it could begin. "I believe he has a very sensitive soul, and Elinor struggles to understand such."

"I am not beyond understanding!" Elinor cried.

"Oh, not on most things, but you do struggle to accept those who are different from you," Marianne continued. "How often do you feel utterly at a loss as to how best to help me? I know it is true. I have heard you sigh. You long to be useful and yet, in those moments you know not how, and it cuts your heart, for you are a very good and loving sister. I could not see you condemned to such sorrow for all your life just so that you could marry a gentleman as handsome as Colonel Brandon. I am certain I would perish from the guilt of having caused you unhappiness if I were to promote such a match and be successful. Therefore, I could not in good conscience do anything else but inform him that Mrs. Jennings is incorrect. You and he would not suit."

There was a lot of truth in her argument, but she knew that the reasons she stated were not her only reasons. There was another reason she wished for Colonel Brandon to not consider Elinor, although she could not quite put her finger on what it was. However, whether she could name it or not, she knew there was at least one more reason why she absolutely could not promote a match between the colonel and Elinor.

"And you think you would suit him better?" Elinor asked.

Marianne gasped. That was it! That was the other reason. She wanted Colonel Brandon to consider her. It all made perfect sense now – the pricking of her heart, her desire to prove him wrong in his thinking that he was too old for her, the disappointment that had settled on her when he spoke of seeing her matched with another – they were, of course, all signs that her heart had chosen him and needed him to chose her in return.

She looked up from the music that was spread across the top of her instrument. "Do you think I would?" she asked.

"He is old," Margaret answered. "He will be gouty and die within ten years."

"Margaret!" her mother scolded.

"It is what happens to old men," Margaret reasoned.

"It does not," Elinor chided.

"He does have a pain in his leg," Marianne said,

"but it is from an injury sustained in battle, so it must be forgiven and not credited to his age."

"He was injured in battle?" There was a reverence to Margaret's tone.

Marianne nodded. "He was knocked off his horse, and his leg was broken."

Margaret sighed. "We must meet him, Mama!"

"You are not to ask him about his injuries," her mother cautioned.

"Oh, I promise I will not," Margaret said. "Please, might we meet him?"

Her mother smiled and shook her head. "I suppose there is no other way to determine if he and Marianne would suit."

Margaret clapped her hands and scooted over to the piano just as Marianne began to play. "If you marry him," Margaret whispered, "might I then ask him about his injuries?"

"Margaret!" Marianne chided in a stern whisper, but then added with a small smile. "So long as Elinor and Mama do not hear you."

Chapter 4

Later that day, as the sun passed its height and began its descent, and after Marianne had completed many of her tasks for the day, she and Margaret slipped out the back door of Barton Cottage, intent upon finding a short moment of refreshment that could only be truly found in a walk.

"Do you think we will meet Colonel Brandon?" Margaret asked.

"I should think not," Marianne replied, though she secretly hoped they might. She had thought of little else all day other than if Colonel Brandon would like the music she played, if he had read the book she was reading, if the picture she was painting would be to his taste, if he preferred large gardens or small, and how he would look sitting near the window in the sitting room with a cup of tea in his hand and a charming, pensive look on his face. It seemed as if he had filled every corner of her mind.

"Well, I hope we do." The words were tossed over Margaret's shoulder as she skipped ahead. Stopping, she turned back toward Marianne. "Do you think it will rain? The clouds are very heavy."

Marianne knew that being caught in the rain, something both Elinor and Mama cautioned them against, was a favourite thing for her daring youngest sister. "If we are, we mustn't get too wet, or Elinor will scold."

Margaret's nose wrinkled as her lips pursed. "And Mama will make us drink that horrid tea."

"We will stand under a tree if needed."

Marianne had no desire to drink Mama's horrid tea or catch a chill since the first was unpleasant and the second would mean not being able to leave her room and missing many chances to see Colonel Brandon. It would be lovely to have him call and inquire after her health, of course, but to have to lie in bed while knowing he was entertaining Elinor was not something she wished to have to endure.

As those heavy clouds would have it, Marianne and Margaret did indeed find themselves standing under a large tree as sheets of rain fell on the ground around the tree's dense canopy with very few drops making their way through the leaves near the trunk where they stood.

"Blast!" A gentleman slipped as he descended the hill in front of where they stood.

"Are you well?" Marianne called. She hoped he was because she did not relish the idea of having to leave her place and venture into the downpour to help him.

"Yes," he called back as he picked himself up off the ground and continued running toward them. "Only my pride is damaged," he added as he joined them under the tree. "Do you have room for one more in your leafy fortress?"

Margaret giggled and assured him that they did.

"Mr. John Willoughby at your service," he said with a bow before taking up a position next to the tree's trunk. "And who might I have the pleasure of meeting?"

"I am Miss Marianne Dashwood, and this is my sister, Miss Margaret Dashwood."

"Dashwood, you say? I had heard there was a new family at Barton Cottage named Dashwood – a lady and her three beautiful daughters, as it was told to me. You obviously must be two of those beauties, for even the greyness of the day seems lessened in your presence."

They were very pretty words, and Marianne could not help but feel them profoundly. A lady always enjoyed being told she was beautiful.

"We just arrived at Barton Cottage," Margaret assured their companion. "It is much smaller than Norland, which is where we used to live, but it has Mama, so it is perfect, really."

Perfect was not precisely the word Marianne would use for Barton Cottage. However, she could agree with Margaret that it was small and made that much more bearable because their mother was there.

Still, she missed Norland and its large, bright rooms and fine fittings. However, she did not miss her brother's wife, who had become the mistress of Norland in their mother's place after their father had died, and the absence of Fanny Dashwood was the one thing that made Barton Cottage preferable to Norland.

No, that was no longer true she thought with a smile. There was now also Colonel Brandon. His presence in the area made Barton Cottage quite desirable as a place to live.

"You are the second gentleman I have met today when wandering these hills," Marianne said to Willoughby. "I shall have to make it a habit to walk here often, so that I might make more friends. You are from the area, are you not, Mr. Willoughby?"

Willoughby chuckled. "Indeed, I am. My aunt has an estate not far from here. It will be mine eventually." He turned to rest just his shoulder against the tree as he spoke to her. "Besides myself, whom might you have been fortunate enough to stumble upon today?"

"Colonel Brandon," Margaret answered. "Although I did not meet him. I have only met you. But Marianne met him and told me about him, so I am eager to make his acquaintance."

"Brandon is at Barton Park!" Their companion seemed to shift uneasily. "I had not heard he had arrived."

"I think he has only just arrived," Marianne said.

"I wonder how long he will stay?" Willoughby mumbled.

"He did not say," Marianne answered even though she was certain he was not asking to get a reply but rather just thinking aloud. "However, I can ask him tonight when we dine with Sir John."

"Oh, oh, look!" Margaret cried. "We *should* walk in the rain more often, Marianne. Look, it is Sir John, and someone is with him. Is it the colonel?"

"Well, speak of the devil," Willoughby muttered.

"Yes," Marianne answered her sister with a curious look at Willoughby, "that is Colonel Brandon."

"A right old bore if ever there was one," Willoughby said. "But a pleasant enough fellow."

"A bore?" Marianne said in surprise. "I did not think such about him when we met." She had not found one thing about the colonel that seemed boring.

Willoughby shrugged. "It happens as one grows older they say." He lowered his voice. "He has a child."

"He does not!" Marianne cried.

"Oh, he does, although he does not claim her as his child but rather his ward. I met her this past season in Bath. That is how I know the colonel to be a bore. It is through her account. He was dead set against her travelling to Bath for some time. She had to work on him most diligently to be allowed to go. He'd rather she stayed home and did her studies and nothing else, for he wishes for her to be a governess or to find a position at a school."

"He does not want her to marry?" Margaret asked in surprise.

"He is not married himself. I doubt he places much value in the institution, but, seeing as he will not claim her as his, she has very little standing, you know. He will, of course, have some coin set aside for her, but she said he had no desire to promote her to society."

"How dreadful!" Margaret cried. "How old is she?"

"Sixteen perhaps," Willoughby replied.

"That is almost how old Marianne is!"

"Margaret!" Marianne chided. She did not like what Mr. Willoughby was saying and was feeling very much like Elinor at the moment, which made it impossible for her to approve of Margaret's entering into gossip so readily. Colonel Brandon was not a dishonorable bore. He could not be. Could he be?

"Miss Marianne! Miss Margaret!" Sir John greeted them in his normal jovial fashion. "I see you have also been caught out in this weather as we have. Willoughby," he gave a nod of greeting to their companion. "Have you met Colonel Brandon?"

"I have," Marianne said with a smile for the colonel. "Just this morning, but Margaret has not."

"You know Willoughby," Sir John said to Colonel Brandon, "and apparently Miss Marianne, though you had not told me you met her."

There was that teasing wink Sir John favoured. This time, however, Marianne did not mind having it directed at her.

"Allow me to introduce you to her sister, Miss Margaret," Sir John continued. "With any luck, you will meet their mother and sister this evening."

"Oh, indeed you will!" Margaret cried. "Mama sent back an acceptance of your invitation, Sir John."

"Capital news! I shall look forward to seeing it when I return home." He turned toward Willoughby. "I see by your empty hands you have been as successful as we have been, but then we were doing more talking than is advisable when stalking prey, were we not, Brandon?"

"We were," the colonel answered.

"And yet you did not mention meeting Miss Marianne."

"I had not had the opportunity to do so. It did not seem like the thing to just toss into a conversation about hunting and dogs."

Marianne enjoyed the serious look on the colonel's face, coupled with the twinkle of amusement in his eyes. If one were to study him, one would likely find much that was interesting. However, if not observing carefully, one would only hear his tone and see his set expression and miss the hidden nuances. No matter what Mr. Willoughby or some supposed daughter of the colonel's said, Colonel Brandon was not a bore. Not to her. But then, she was more curious than most.

"The rain is thankfully slowing," Sir John continued. "It was quite the deluge there for a few minutes. If we were not so very wet, I would offer to see you and Miss Margaret home."

"I do not mind a little rain," Marianne replied. If Sir John and Colonel Brandon did not see them home, then Mr. Willoughby would think it was his duty and frankly, anyone who thought Colonel Brandon was a bore was not someone with whom

Marianne wished to spend a great deal of time. "But I am equally as confident that we can find our way home on our own. Can we not, Margaret?"

Margaret's brow furrowed, and Marianne gave her a pleading look.

"Of course, we are not lost." Margaret's expression softened as Marianne smiled at her in relief.

"If you do not mind a bit of rain," the colonel offered, "I have not forgotten the way to Barton Cottage and would be pleased to make certain you arrived there in safety. However, I will not be able to stay. We have a dinner for which to prepare, and we have the dogs."

"Then we would be happy for the assistance," Marianne replied quickly.

"We could make it a merry party," Willoughby added.

Was he insisting on joining them? The thought annoyed Marianne. "I see no reason to delay you from your purpose, Mr. Willoughby."

"It is not a delay. The rain has put an end to any purpose I might have had."

Marianne pulled her lips into what she hoped was a bright smile. "Then, shall we be on our way?"

Thankfully, the colonel offered her his arm, leaving Sir John with the dogs and Willoughby to display his gallantry for Margaret. When they reached Barton Cottage, Sir John ducked inside to assure Mrs. Dashwood that he was delighted to hear she would be joining him for dinner at Barton Park. He would send his carriage to collect them at half past four. Mr. Willoughby and the colonel were spoken of and made known to Mrs. Dashwood. Then, Sir John took his leave, and Marianne and Margaret were shuffled off to be warmed, dried, and put into proper clothes for dining.

Chapter 5

Marianne sighed with delight as she savoured a bite of chocolate tart. The meal tonight at Barton Park had been exceptional. The items offered were exactly the same, with a few variances, as what had been offered last week, but tonight they were enjoyed in the presence of Colonel Brandon.

It was not only the food that was more delicious due to the colonel's presence. Marianne was certain Sir John had spoken of hunting just as much last week as this, but he had done so with only himself to be interested. Today, the colonel's input made the discussion much more enjoyable.

"Mr. Willoughby is a fine-looking young man," Mrs. Jennings said with a pointed look at Marianne. "His inheritance is good."

"If he has any left when he receives it," muttered

the colonel, who was seated just across from her and down one chair.

"What is that you said, Colonel?" Mrs. Jennings asked.

"I believe he questions the man's ability to keep his finances in order," said Sir John.

"Forgive me," the colonel said, looking rather uneasy, "you know I do not like to tell tales."

"But if you have started one," Mrs. Jennings said with an eager smile, "then you must finish, or I will have to concoct my own version."

Marianne watched with interest as the colonel gave Mrs. Jennings a tight smile and took a sip of his wine before replying. He was, no doubt, calculating his words before he spoke. She smiled behind her glass. That was very clever of him to do it in such a fashion that it seemed like a natural pause.

"I have heard he enjoys the finer things in life as many young gentlemen with no occupation do."

"Indeed?" Mrs. Jennings' brows rose. "He does wear a suit of clothes well. Would you not agree, Miss Marianne?"

Marianne nearly choked on her wine. "I had not considered it."

She cast a worried look in the colonel's direction. It would not do for him to think she found Mr. Willoughby to be a person of interest. She had still not finished convincing Colonel Brandon that she should be a person of interest to him. Indeed! She had only just realized she should persuade him of such, and to have him thinking she fancied some other gentleman would be a setback before she even began on her task in earnest.

"Oh, come, Miss Marianne. Every young lady notices the cut of a gentleman's coat," Mrs. Jennings insisted.

"His coat was very fine," Margaret supplied.

"See," Mrs. Jennings said. "Miss Margaret noticed, so surely you did as well."

Marianne shook her head. "I am sorry, but I did not. I suppose it was a nice coat. I think I would have noticed if it were not."

"You are a strange young woman," Mrs. Jennings said with a laugh.

"She just might not wish to discuss such things," Elinor interjected.

"A modest girl," Sir John said with a wink. "I say,

if we gents were not present, then you'd have your reply, Madame."

"No," Marianne cried. "I assure you that I took no particular notice of his coat."

She glanced anxiously once again in the colonel's direction. He was resolutely chasing a crumb around his plate. Was it because he did not wish to hear what she had to say because he did not wish for her to be fond of Mr. Willoughby or did it just not matter to him as to what her answer would be?

"His coat is the least of his expenses," the colonel said, looking up from his plate, "but his other expenditures are not fit for polite conversation."

Mrs. Jennings gasped.

"Thank you," Marianne mouthed as the topic of Mr. Willoughby's coat was dropped.

The colonel acknowledged her thanks with a tiny nod of his head and a half smile. He did care about her – at least enough to see that she was not further put upon by a subject that distressed her. However, her elation over such a thing was squelched as Elinor, who was seated beside the colonel, leaned toward him and whispered something that caused him to smile completely, not merely in part.

"Shall we go to the drawing room," Lady Middleton rose, and the other ladies followed suit.

"How do you like our colonel?" Mrs. Jennings asked Elinor. "He would make an excellent husband."

Marianne sucked in a breath. No, no, no. Mrs. Jennings could not be pushing Elinor and the colonel together. That would not do at all.

"He seems pleasant," Elinor said with a glance at Marianne. "However, I fear we might be too much alike."

"Too alike! I never heard such a thing!" Mrs. Jennings cried as Marianne expelled the breath she had been holding, and Elinor hid a small smile.

"Sit with me, Miss Marianne. Now that the gentlemen are not with us, you can tell me what you think of Mr. Willoughby."

"I could not," Marianne protested.

"It is perfectly acceptable," Mrs. Jennings insisted. "Did you not find him handsome?"

"Oh, he was handsome to be sure. I will freely admit that, but there seems to be something wanting, although I could not tell you what it is."

It was true that she could not say what it was, but it was not true that she did not know what was missing about Mr. Willoughby. He was not the colonel, and her heart had decided on the colonel well before — nearly half-a-day before — meeting Mr. Willoughby, and she was not so fickle as to choose two gentlemen on the same day! Indeed, she was not certain she would pick Willoughby in any case. No, that might not be true. Her head tipped as she considered it.

If she had met Mr. Willoughby before she had met Colonel Brandon and had Mr. Willoughby spoken of Sir John being a bore, she might have liked him. Her brow furrowed, but did that mean that her heart was not to be trusted if it only took the time of day and subject of discussion to recommend one gentleman over another? Why would she have accepted Willoughby if things had been different?

She rubbed her heart as it pinched at the thought of choosing Willoughby and never having chosen the colonel. She did not mind the pinch, for it was a reassuring sort of pain which told her that no matter the time of day or topic of discussion, her heart would eventually have found the colonel. She looked up to see Mrs. Jennings watching her.

"Have you deciphered what is wanting?" she asked. "You were in such deep contemplation that surely you must have."

Marianne smiled and shook her head. "I really could not say what it is."

"I think you and he would find much in common," Mrs. Jennings said.

"Then, they would not suit at all," Elinor said, "for they would likely be far too much alike."

"Too much alike? Again?"

Elinor nodded. "If Mr. Willoughby is as given to flights of fancy as my sister is, theirs would not be a very sensible marriage. Somewhat alike is good. Too alike is to be avoided."

"Our colonel was given to passion when he was a young man, or so I have heard," Mrs. Jennings said to Elinor in a persuasive tone. "He might be just enough unlike you for you to suit."

Elinor shook her head. "I am sorry, but I would prefer not to suit."

"Prefer not to suit! Well, I have heard everything tonight. I shall have a time of it to see either of you married."

"Not if it is the right gentleman," Elinor assured her, a faint blush staining her cheeks.

Marianne knew who the right gentleman was, but they had left him behind at Norland. "And only if it is the right time," she said, hoping that her eyes could convey part of the sorrow she felt on Elinor's behalf.

"The right time is any time after you are presented to society and preferably before you are sat on the shelf. It is much harder to find a match the older you get," Mrs. Jennings cautioned.

"I think we have a few years before we will be out of luck," Elinor assured her.

"I would not be too slow in coming to the point," Mrs. Jennings said. "I assure you that a young man can improve with age, Miss Marianne. Why, our colonel has become right serious – nearly too much so – since returning to us, but then, that might be due to the love child. However, I must not speak of such things, for the gentlemen are here."

The love child? Marianne closed her mouth, which had dropped open at Mrs. Jennings's words. Then, it was true that the colonel had a daughter? He must have been a very young man to have a daughter who was nearly the same age as she was.

That must be why he would not speak of the lady he mentioned in the meadow this morning.

"Miss Marianne, you must play for us," Sir John stood before her with his hand outstretched.

Play for them? How could she play for them when her heart was in such a jumbled state? She could not marry the colonel and be a mother to someone who was her own age. She just could not. And therefore, her heart was likely to be forever broken.

However, despite her jumbled brain and troubled heart, she placed her hand in Sir John's and allowed him to lead her to the instrument.

"The colonel will see to your pages," Sir John said with that same teasing wink that so often irritated her.

This time, it threatened to cause tears to fall. How could she play while he, who could never be hers, stood beside her, ready to assist with the moving of pages?

"Are you well?" Colonel Brandon asked as she took her seat.

She shrugged. "I am uncertain if I wish to play or not."

"I thought you enjoyed music?"

"I do, but..." She looked back at Mrs. Jennings before setting aside the song she had hoped to convince the colonel to sing with her in favour of a piece that contained no lyrics.

"What has happened?" he asked quietly as her fingers began to find their way along the instrument.

She shook her head. "I cannot say. Not while I am playing and perhaps not at all."

"There are a few things in my life about which I feel the same. It takes a great deal of fortitude to not think about them too often."

He was watching her face. She could see it out of the corner of her eye. He was so attentive and so kind. Surely, Mrs. Jennings could be wrong, could she not be? Marianne's heart had never wished so vigorously for someone to be incorrect.

"One of those things is Eliza."

Her fingers stumbled over the keys. "Is she?"

He nodded. "The lady I mentioned this morning. I should like to speak to you of her."

"Why?"

He shook his head and sighed deeply. "I do not know exactly. I have not spoken of her in years, but..." He shook his head again. "I do not know. I just do."

"Then I will listen."

"We were star-crossed lovers. It is not a pretty tale."

Marianne blew out a breath, willing her heart to stop its racing. "I am certain I am equal to it," she assured him.

"Tomorrow morning?" he asked.

She nodded. How she would survive until then, she was uncertain. Curiosity was not always a friend.

However, she did survive the night and its copious amounts of tossing and turning. Sometime in the midst of being unsettled and in an attempt to test her heart to see how much agony it could withstand, she had even imagined him telling her about his lost love and the daughter they shared. Therefore, as she climbed the path to the meadow, she was certain her heart was prepared for whatever he might tell her. That is, she was confident of her preparation to hear something dreadful until she saw him and he turned toward her with a bright smile. Then, from the way her heart skipped, she feared she had not prepared it as well as she had hoped.

Chapter 6

"Good morning," Colonel Brandon greeted Marianne as she approached him. "I left Lorcan at Barton Park. I hope you are not disappointed."

"No, I am not." The breeze pushed at her bonnet. His hat was already in his hand. It seemed she had been correct that he did not like to wear it overly much.

"Thomas has accompanied me, however." He nodded toward where his horse stood with his groom and his groom's mount. "I did not wish for my beast to wander away." He extended an arm to her.

She placed her hand on his arm where it felt it belonged. Oh, her heart was not going to survive this if it had to give him up. It was too far gone to be gently pried away.

"The mist was heavy this morning. I feared I

would not be allowed to walk out." Her mother had nearly denied her until she had begged most convincingly that flowers were needed on such a gloomy-looking morning.

"I am glad it lifted some."

"As am I," she agreed.

"Shall I begin?"

She nodded and steeled her heart. She wanted to look away from him. She did not want to see his pain or have him see hers, but she was no coward. Or, at least, she was not for about a minute. Then, she allowed her eyes to wander the path before them.

He blew out a breath. "I am uncertain how to begin. I have attempted to start this conversation many times during the night."

"Then let me help you," Marianne said softly. "Who is Eliza?"

"Eliza was my cousin, who grew up with me. Her parents died when she was just an infant, and my father was her guardian. There was only a year difference in our age, so as you can well imagine we were great playfellows and friends. I cannot remember a time when I did not love Eliza.

"That love grew as we grew, and at one time, I

had purposed to take her for my wife. My father, however, had purposed to give her and her fortune to my brother, so that the estate would no longer languish." He shook his head and paused for a moment.

"We had schemed to escape to Scotland, but we were discovered. I was sent away to stay with a distant relation, while Eliza was confined at home until my father's point had been gained, and she was married to my brother."

Marianne sucked in a sharp breath. How horrid! To have lost his love to another would be tragic indeed, but to have always had to be reminded of that loss when he saw her with his brother must have been unbearable.

"Was she eventually happy?"

He shook his head. "My brother was unkind to her. He only accepted her for her money, and for a time, she bore the situation, though unhappily. Eventually, however, she could withstand no more, and, after seeking some form of love in the arms of someone who was not my brother, the marriage was put to an end."

He ceased speaking, and they walked on for several minutes in silence.

"I was in the East Indies when I heard of the dissolution of their marriage two years after it had happened. You have no way of knowing the grief and gloom that overtook me at the news. I had left, so that she might have some hope of finding happiness without my presence constantly reminding her of what could have been. Had I known, I never would have left."

"You could not know," Marianne rushed to reassure him. "You did what you thought was right and what should have been right. The sins of your father or brother or even your dear Eliza are not yours to bear."

He smiled at her sadly. "I have told myself that many times."

"Then you should listen to yourself, for it is sound advice."

He covered the hand that lay on his arm with his free one. "So I should, but I fear I feel the weight of it all too greatly. I returned to England, but not before she had fallen into desperate circumstances. I found her in a poorhouse, sick and not at all as I remembered."

He fell silent again, and Marianne, who could

only imagine the agony he must be remembering, squeezed his arm reassuringly.

"She was not long in living after my return, but I visited her as often as I could." He drew and released a breath. "She had a daughter. The child was three when I found her mother."

"Oh." The word leapt from Marianne's mouth. "The child is not yours?"

"No, I do not know her father. Eliza would never name him."

"But you care for her?"

His brow furrowed. "I do, but how do you know?"

Marianne looked down at the ground where they had stopped and now stood. "Mr. Willoughby mentioned having met your daughter in Bath."

"Willoughby?"

Marianne nodded.

"Did he only meet her once?"

"I could not say except that he spoke as if they had met often."

"Did he say if he had seen her recently?"

Marianne shook her head. "Why?"

He turned away from her and looked up to the sky for a moment before turning back as he scrubbed his face with his hands. "I have attempted to see to her care and education. I promised her dying mother that I would. I sent her to school, but eventually, I removed her from there to place her with a very respectable woman. And all was well for a time, so I allowed her to go to Bath with one of her friends who was also in this lady's care. It was a mistake, for she disappeared from there. I have not heard from or of her since."

"She is missing?" Marianne's hand covered her rapidly beating heart at the shock of such a thing.

He nodded.

"And her friend did not know where she was?"

"She would not tell me, though I believe she knew all."

"How could she not tell you?" Marianne cried. "This is a dreadful business, indeed! We must find her." Marianne flushed as he tipped his head to look at her curiously.

"I mean you," Marianne corrected. "You must find her."

"I have attempted, and still I search, but all to no avail." He took her hand, his eyes searching hers. "I know what the whispers are about my relationship to her."

"But they are untrue," Marianne said firmly.

"That will not make them go away."

"They matter not."

"I fear loving again." He dropped her hand and turned away from her. "I failed my Eliza, and now I have failed her daughter. I can only imagine that she has eloped or fallen into the same destitute position as her mother."

"Does she love you? Eliza's daughter? What is her name?"

He shrugged. "Her name is Eliza after her mother."

"Does young Eliza love you?"

"I thought she did."

Marianne moved to stand next to him and placed her hand on his arm. "Could she have done something about which she fears telling you?"

His eyes were on her hand where it lay on his arm. "It is possible."

"Then it is even more imperative that we find her." She sucked in a breath and lifted her eyes to him. "However I might be able to help you, you have only to ask."

"Why?"

Marianne looked out at the meadow before her

where the mist was lifting to reveal the freshness of the grass and flowers that lay beneath it.

"Because I cannot bear to see you in such pain any more than you can bear to speak of your Eliza's demise with equanimity." She looked at him and shrugged. "I am young and likely foolish – or so Elinor claims often."

She smiled at his tentatively hopeful expression. "And though I have no experience in these things aside from what I have read or been told, I believe I love you."

She was sure her heart was about to climb up her throat and escape her body before she did something more to send it racing even faster than it was at this moment.

"We have only met, and I am an old man compared to you," he protested even as he brushed a wayward tendril of hair from her cheek.

"You are not an old man," she returned with a shake of her head. "Not to me." Again, she shook her head. "I do not understand it all myself, but my heart has chosen you. I wish to see you happy, to see you gathering flowers, and to hear you singing, and I also wish to hold your hand and reassure you when life has dealt you an agonising blow such as this present loss of Eliza."

"I am not an easy man," he argued.

"I am not an easy lady," she countered. "I am prone to fits of temper at times, and I do love the fanciful more often than Elinor can tolerate." She took his hand in hers. "I have no fortune, nor do I have a father. The only estate I have ever known was taken from me by a brother. I have not a lot to offer you besides my heart."

"I do not deserve such a precious gift." He lifted her hand to his lips and kissed it softly. "I fear you will vanish with the mist that brought you to me."

"Never," she replied.

He looked up to the clouds above them and drew a deep breath. "The sun is shining."

What a beautiful smile he had! It demanded she respond in kind while saying, "It is," in agreement with him. It was certainly shining on his face.

He lifted her hand to his heart and shook his head. "Not just in the sky. Here. I had feared it never would until yesterday when I met you. And then I feared it was only a glimpse sent to torture me by reminding me of what I have lost."

Marianne wondered if any lady had ever felt as

treasured as she felt at that moment with him looking down at her.

He cupped her cheek with his hand. "May I kiss you?"

"You may," she said, but added as he gathered her into his embrace, "as long as you promise me that you will believe that only when the morning mist fails to appear, only then, will I stop reminding you of my admiration for you."

"It will take some time," he replied, "but I shall do my best to not doubt that you will be snatched from me."

"Then, you must kiss me."

And he did, holding her to him as if she were a precious jewel in need of protection while his lips pressed against hers, tentatively at first, until Marianne sighed with pleasure. Then, as Marianne wound her finger in his hair, he deepened the kiss, speaking to her without words about the amorous man who lay behind his composed facade and declaring himself to be a gentleman who loved her as none other could.

As the last tendrils of the morning mist raced away, followed by the playful pixies that caused a lady to shiver in the coolness of a fresh, new day, Marianne's heart found its home. It was not in an estate or a cottage, but in the love of a gallant gentleman who was as noble as any knight of old and who would love her until his eyes would close, never to see the morning mist rise from a meadow again.

Theirs would be a love that would surpass anything the colonel had ever imagined possible and of which Marianne had ever dreamt. For while they were not too alike in all things, for he was serious while she was fanciful, there was one trait which they shared – a passion that was incapable of loving by halves.

Frosted
Windowpanes

Just like the frost brings beauty to the coldness of winter,
beauty can rise out of sorrow

Chapter 1

Patrick Mullins flipped up his collar and pulled it closer around his neck. There was a definite December bite to the evening air, but he was in no hurry to escape it as some others seemed to be. He stepped to the side as a pair of ladies dressed in woolen coats, attempting to escape the chill, hurried past him, clinging closely to each other. A man, moving at a steady pace – neither hurried nor relaxed – and carrying a small crate on his shoulder — passed with a cheerful "pardon me" before he continued whistling a tune, each note being made visible by the chilly air. The light from lanterns recently lit by a faithful lamplighter created pools of light here and there along the high street and chased away all the shadows that dared creep near the edge of their light-filled pools. To Patrick, it was a cheery, welcoming sight. How he had missed this! This was home, and no matter what painful memories this place might hold, it was where he belonged. He would not leave again.

When he had first received the news of his brother's accident, he had thought he would be coming back here only to dispose of some property in such a fashion as to secure himself a life of relative ease elsewhere – anywhere but here. However, he had had ample time to consider his future during his voyage.

Ashmore Lodge called to him, and he could not deny it. It was where generations of ancestors resided in portraits and lived on in stories handed down from one generation to the next. He could not dispose of his family. He had left them four years ago, but not because he had wanted to. No, he had left them out of necessity. As a second son, his lot in life was to earn his fortune. He had written to his brother and mother faithfully. Though he had been absent when both had been called to the life beyond this one, he had never turned his back on them, and he would not now.

He thanked the lad who brought him his horse and swung himself up into the saddle. He had considered staying at the Rose and Crown tonight and making his way to Ashmore Lodge in the morning, but, he smiled to himself, he had never been a patient man. So instead, he had availed himself of a hearty meal and a stout pint of ale and was now set to make the short journey to Ashmore Lodge a day ahead of schedule.

"Mr. Mullins."

Patrick turned toward the person who called him. "Philip!" he cried in surprise. "You are Philip Dobney, are you not?" He dismounted and stuck a hand out in greeting to his friend.

Philip Dobney laughed and shook the hand extended to him heartily. "A bit older, a little stouter, but in essentials, still me. Of course, you remember my wife, Lucy?"

Patrick tipped his hat and smiled. "I remember Miss Tolson, but I have never met Mrs. Dobney, although I had heard that Philip had been fortunate enough to secure himself a bride."

"It is I who am the fortunate one," Lucy replied with a smile as she leaned into Philip's arm. "You did hear the whole story, did you not?"

While one of Lucy's hands was tucked in the crook of her husband's arm, the other rested on her rather round belly. It seemed his old friends were soon to become parents. A pang of jealousy shot through Patrick. Four years ago, he had hoped to be as fortunate as Philip currently was. If *she* had stayed true to her word, he could have been a father by now.

"I did," Patrick replied. "Or, at least, I believe I did. My mother was an excellent correspondent, and my brother was only slightly less good. However, I am unaware if there were any bits and pieces they left out. Allow me to extend my sympathy on the passing of your father, late though it is in coming."

His mother had told him how Lucy's father had died, leaving his estate to his brother, a good-for-nothing sort of fellow, and how Lucy had struck a bargain with Philip to be his wife rather than endure life with her uncle. The story had not ended there. There had been much that followed that – a twisted, sorted sort of tale that he had had a hard time believing was capable of playing out in the sleepy town of Kympton.

"Philip and I would be delighted to share the whole of it with you over tea at some point if you wish," Lucy replied. "The Lord has been good to us."

"I can see that," Patrick answered. The pair before him looked as happy as any couple he had ever seen.

"Good can come out of tragedy," Lucy continued, looking at Patrick with that pointed look he remembered so well.

Lucy Tolson had often used that look when she had something to say but was too gentle to say it bluntly. She apparently expected some good to come from his current situation. He hoped she was right, for his life for the past four years had been good, but it had never been truly happy.

"Our condolences on the passing of both your mother and brother," she added. "It is not a happy event that has returned you to us, but we are glad to have you back."

"Indeed, we are," Philip said eagerly. "You will find much changed around here."

"I am certain I will."

"But do not let us keep you from your journey," Lucy said. "I am not certain anyone expects you to arrive at Ashmore tonight."

There was a sparkle to her eyes as if she knew something he did not.

"I am entirely too impatient to see the place,"

Patrick replied. "Is there anything I should know before I arrive at home?"

Home. He drew and released a breath at the word. It felt right to finally be at home.

The sparkle in Lucy's eye did not fade as she shook her head. "Not a thing. I think you will find it relatively unchanged and ready to receive you." Her lips pursed as if she was attempting to contain a smile.

There was likely some surprise waiting for him at Ashmore, and Lucy had probably had a hand in it. He would not press her for the details. He would simply ride home and enjoy whatever it was that awaited him, then tell her about his delight the next time he saw her.

"Well, then, I suppose I will be on my way."

"Welcome home," Philip said, giving Patrick's hand one more firm shake before allowing him to mount his horse and ride away.

~*~*~

It was not an excessively long ride to Ashmore. The roads were good for this time of year, and the lack of clouds in the sky meant that, even though the moon was not full, there was still ample light to illuminate his way. Patrick was grateful for that.

For though he was confident he could have made the journey in the dark of a new moon, it was reassuring to be able to see familiar landmarks along the way and know that he had not forgotten as much as he feared he might have over the past four years.

"Can I be of service?" a groom asked as he exited the stables at Patrick's approach. "Master Patrick?" the man said in surprise as he lifted his lantern high to see to whom it was he spoke. "We did not expect you until tomorrow." He leaned to the side and looked behind Patrick. "Is there a carriage?"

"No, it is just me. The rest will arrive tomorrow as planned." Patrick slid off his horse. "It is good to see you, John."

"We are pleased to have you returned," the groom replied before turning and shouting, "It's the master," to a fellow groom just exiting the stables. "Come. Take his horse."

"I see you still run a tight ship," Patrick said with a chuckle. "John's not too harsh a master, is he?" he asked as he relinquished the reins he held to the lad who had scampered at John's barking to do as he was told.

"No, sir. He is right kind."

"And whom might you be?"

"I be Henry, sir."

"Have you been with us long?"

"No, sir, only two months."

Two months. Not long enough to have been here when his brother, Fredrick, was. Henry must be one of the replacements for the men who were lost with Fredrick and his mother in the accident.

"And a good hand he is," John said. "He's taken up well where others left off."

So, he was correct. This young lad, who looked to be no more than fourteen, had come to Ashmore after the accident.

"I am glad to hear it." He gave a nod to the lad and allowed him to continue with his work instead of standing there waiting for Patrick to question him further.

"It is good to have you home, sir," John repeated, a smile gracing his face for a moment before sobering. "Not for the reasons it was necessary, of course."

"No one ever wishes to be called home for such a reason." Patrick turned and looked toward the house. "I had hoped to eventually return to my family with tales of adventure." He shook his head. "I have the tales. It is just the family I lack."

"I've always got a ready ear," John said quietly. "I know it is not the same, but until you have formed a new family, my ear is available."

Patrick clapped the older man on the shoulder. John had been at Ashmore for at least fifteen years. He was as much part of the estate family as anyone. "You are a good man, John, and I might take you up on that offer at some point." He clapped his hands and rubbed them together eagerly, an impish smile on his face. "Now, do you wish to go with me when I surprise Mrs. White?"

John chuckled. "No. I shall stay here where it is safe."

"Lacking bravery, are you?" Patrick teased.

"I assure you I have courage aplenty. I just am not lacking in good sense. I like my meals without cross words and harsh glares. I'll have no part of taking the blame for your tampering with Mrs. White's schedule."

Patrick laughed. "I am no stranger to her displeasure, but I see your point. Wish me well."

When he was young, Patrick had often found many ways to torment the housekeeper. He'd move things from place to place, steal a key when it was within his reach, and stamp his boots inside the door rather than making use of the brush outside.

He had eventually *nearly* outgrown such impishness before he left home, and then the past four years had driven out the rest. However, now that he was home and no longer under the command of another, he felt a bit of that carefree boy returning.

Coming upon the garden, Patrick decided to take a walk through it before entering the house. As much as he was eager to be inside where it was warm, a part of him dreaded the change that would be so evident by the silence of the place when he did enter. There would be no one to greet him aside from servants.

He approached the doors that led from the library to what had been his mother's favourite part of the garden. A light dusting of snow covered the tops of bushes and bare branches. He stood and looked at them for a few minutes, pondering how they seemed to reflect his own state of being – cold, barren, and waiting. Waiting for what? That was the question. Patrick had no idea what awaited him now. Oh, he knew he would run the estate as well as it could be run, and come next winter, he would venture to town to attempt to secure a bride, so that he could do his part to provide a son or two who could continue to care for Ashmore when he was gone. However, beyond those things, and because of those things, he felt very unsure of himself.

He looked at the house. His home. The place that was now his responsibility. He would do his best by it.

The glass panes in the library doors were painted with the intricate white designs of Jack Frost and his legion of pixies. Those designs, his mother had said, were a reminder to Patrick that even in the coldest of winter weather and at the darkest time of the year, there was still beauty to be found.

It sounded very much like what Lucy had said to him earlier about beauty being found in tragedy. Once again, he hoped that something good could be found in all of this. He sighed and walked closer to the doors where he traced one of the patterns left by the frost. As he did, the room before him lit with the soft glow of one candle and then another and another.

Every ounce of breath he had in his lungs

escaped him in a great whoosh as the lighter of the candles came into view. It was *her*. Illuminated by the glow of the candle she held, and framed by the soft and delicate designs of the frost on the windowpanes of the library doors, was Amanda, looking every bit as beautiful as he remembered her.

Chapter 2

Amanda Thompson moved lightly around the library, placing the books she carried on a table near Patrick's favourite chair, checking the shelves, and straightening anything that she decided was out of place while Patrick stood transfixed, rooted to the frozen ground beneath his feet.

He had known that eventually they would have to meet, but he had hoped it would not be for some time. Dealing with the newness of his recently acquired position in life while grieving anew the loss of his family would be difficult enough without being reminded of his shortcomings by the lady who had tossed him aside, crushing his heart with her refusal – a heart which still longed for her all these years later.

He had attempted to find someone else to take her place in his affections, but it was a fruitless, frustrating business. No one had ever laughed as she did. None had smiled quite like her. Not a single young lady he had met had been able to converse with him on things which he held dear as she used to do.

She approached the doors, most likely to check the lock and draw the drapes across to help keep the chill of the night from entering the room. Her lips formed an *o* as her eyes grew wide, and she stopped mid-stride when she saw him.

Patrick jiggled the door handle. It was locked as expected. He could dash around the house and enter through the door, but then there would be servants to greet and such. Amanda, the lady about whom he had dreamt for four years, was here, and though it was surprising and unsettling to see her so directly upon arriving, he had no wish to allow her to escape before he could hear her voice in reality instead of just in his dreams. Therefore, he gave the door handle another jiggle and motioned for her to open it for him.

She looked behind her, causing him to think that perhaps she would ignore his request, but she did not.

"Mr. Mullins," she greeted as she opened the door to him.

"Miss Thompson," he replied, stepping into his home and closing the door behind him. It felt odd to hear her name falling from his lips in a tone that was not a painful whisper. It was almost as odd a sensation as standing here in this room, of all places, with her was.

"We had not expected you until tomorrow." She stepped aside and away from him.

"I wished to sleep in my own bed," he answered. He drew in a breath and looked around the room. He could hear noises from somewhere in the house, yet, it still seemed so silent.

"It is not the same, is it?" she asked quietly. "We had hoped to help, at least a little, by making certain everything was just as your mother and brother would have liked it." She dipped her head. "I am very sorry that they are not here to greet you."

"No more than I am," he replied.

"Oh, Patrick." Her hand rested on her heart, and her eyes glistened with unshed tears.

He looked past her to whatever stood behind her, not that he was, in fact, looking at anything in particular. He just could not look at her for he longed to wrap her in his embrace and feel some sort of comfort. "Who is we?" he asked as he began to remove his outerwear.

"Your friends. At least, I hope I can still be part of that group."

He smiled tightly and nodded. This must be the surprise Lucy had known he would find.

"We must begin somewhere I suppose," he answered, "and friends seems to be as good a place to start as anywhere." Having removed his outerwear, he draped it across a nearby chair and began a slow circuit of the small room. "Surely, you are not here alone." He cast a questioning look in her direction.

"No, Mother is in the housekeeper's room. She wanted to make certain that you would not need to trouble yourself with menu selections for at least two weeks." Amanda turned in her spot, following him with her eyes as he moved around the room. "Was your voyage good?"

Patrick took a book from the shelf and paged through it. He had no clue as to what book he held. He just needed something other than her on which to focus. "It was not terrible. Cold, windy, and wet, but we encountered no major storms and had very few days of poor weather."

"I am glad to hear it."

The room fell into an awkward silence. Patrick glanced at her as he returned the book to the shelf. There was plenty he wished to say, but little he felt he should.

"You are probably anxious to get settled into your room," she moved toward the door. "I will tell Mrs. White that you will require some tea and supper."

"Are you married?" He blurted before she could leave the room. He half hoped she would say she was. Then he would have to tell his heart that all was lost instead of allowing it to contemplate a second chance with her.

"What? No!" She turned toward him.

"Neither my brother nor my mother had mentioned anything about a wedding, but then, they did not..." He shrugged.

"They did not speak of me?"

He shook his head. "Why should they?" He tried to keep his tone friendly, but from the way she recoiled, he knew he had not succeeded.

"Why should they not? We have known each

other since we were born! Our families have always been close. Even while you were away, we still gathered as we used to do."

"Indeed?"

"Did your mother never mention it?"

"Never."

"She spoke often enough about you." Amanda folded her arms and tipped her head as she glared at him. "Painfully often."

"I do not see how a mention of me could cause *you* pain." He pressed his lips together. He had not meant to say that, nor had he intended to feel bitterness rising within him. He thought he had overcome that. "Forgive me. I believe my journey has tired me more than I thought. I should see myself to my room."

To his surprise, he saw a spark of fury in her eyes. She was angry? At him? *She* had no reason to be put out with *him*.

"Please," she said with a wave toward the door, "do not let me detain you."

His brow furrowed. Her tone was indeed angry.

"Just do not remain there for four years," she snapped before throwing the door open and exiting hastily.

He rushed after her. "What do you mean by that?"

"Is that not what you did the last time we talked in the library? You decided our conversation was over and that was it. I never heard from you or saw you again until today." Tears glistened in her eyes. "I tried to write to you, but Mother would not allow it."

The mention of her mother not permitting something was more than he could countenance. Had her mother not interfered four years ago, Amanda might have been his. The bitterness that had started to rise before surfaced in all its ugly glory.

"There is not much to discuss when the lady to whom you have offered your heart recants her decision because you are not good enough for her." He shook his head. "I was wrong. It may not be possible for us to remain friends. Miss Thompson, I thank you for the effort you have put into my homecoming. It is not unappreciated, but I find I must go." He bowed and left her, staring wide-eyed and open-mouthed after him.

~*~*~

Patrick slowed his pace when he reached the top

of the stairs. Slowly, he walked down the hall pausing for a moment in front of the doors to what had been his mother's and brother's rooms to remember each of them in turn. Naturally, sadness filled him as he stood in front of each door, but the exercise was necessary. A wily enemy such as grief had to be faced, for what soldier claimed victory over his enemy by hiding?

From the bitterness which had sprung up within him so quickly when speaking with Amanda, Patrick knew the answer to that question quite well. He had hidden from his disappointment for some time – No! That was not entirely true. He had hidden, but he had not *just* hidden. He had fled the field, retreating to what he thought would be a safe distance, only to find reminders of his disappointment in every fair-haired beauty or happily married couple.

He crossed from the door of his room to the writing desk that stood in front of the window and lit the lamp.

"She sat there when she wrote to you."

He turned to find Mrs. Thompson at his door. He had little desire to see her since he still held her in his mind as the source of his unhappy single state.

"Your mother was writing that letter," she indicated the paper he had picked up from the desk, "before she left for town. It did not make sense to send it to you after what happened. You and it would have likely crossed paths and been headed in opposite directions. So, I left it where she had. I knew you would want to read it. Indeed, after reading it myself, I knew you *needed* to read it."

Mrs. Thompson took a seat on the trunk which stood at the end of Patrick's bed.

"Go ahead. Read it."

"Now?"

She nodded. "I would allow you some time and privacy, but my daughter is once again weeping because of you, and I am feeling uncharitable."

"Amanda is crying?" He knew he had been harsh, but he had not expected her to dissolve into tears over a repetition of what she had said to him four years ago when rejecting him.

"Weeping, not crying," Mrs. Thompson corrected. "Now, read."

Patrick did as instructed.

"I will not allow her to pine away for another year. She is four and twenty and soon will be firmly on the shelf," Mrs. Thompson said as Patrick read similar words from his mother. She blew out a breath. "We had all hoped you would come to your senses before now."

Patrick looked up from the letter. "Come to my senses? About what?"

"The fact that you were too young to marry four years ago."

Patrick pulled out the chair next to the desk and sank into it. "I do not follow your meaning."

"You had no career – only the promise of one, and therefore, no income and no way to support a wife and child in a fashion that would provide comfort to them. That is why I counselled Amanda to not accept your offer until you had become better established."

Patrick felt as if he had taken a blow to the abdomen. "Amanda said I was not capable of being a good husband." He sank back into his chair. That was all he had heard. He was not good enough. If there had been any further explanation, he had not listened to it.

"She also told you that she knew you would

succeed in whatever you chose to do," Mrs. Thompson added.

Had she? Patrick searched his memory. There it was. A mumbled jumble of words that had followed her proclamation that he was not worthy of her. "I thought she was attempting to be kind in sending me on my way."

Mrs. Thompson rose and crossed to where he sat. Laying her hand on his shoulder, she said, "We knew that you had not heard things as you should have when you came flying out of the library that night, but I was certain that in the morning, when your disappointment had faded some, you would be able to hear what was being said. However, before Amanda and I could call on you the following day, you were gone."

"Why did you not write?" He looked up at her. The agony that could have been saved if someone had told him this information four years ago.

"That was perhaps a mistake on our part."

He shook his head in bewilderment. That was saying it gently!

"You had asked your mother not to mention Amanda to you. We – your mother and I – thought that eventually, you would ask about her, and then we would broach the subject."

"Four years!"

She nodded sadly. "You always were obstinate."

He shook his head again. For four years his mother and Mrs. Thompson had withheld this information from him. "I both longed and dreaded to hear about her. Because of my dread, I never asked."

"Then you do still love her?"

"I have attempted not to," he admitted.

"Yes, your mother mentioned several of the accounts you shared about this or that young lady. Somehow each one always was wanting for one reason or another."

"They were not Amanda." That was the truth. It had always been the truth. No matter what reason he gave for why he could not pursue a lady, it always came back to this fact. None of them could compare to his Amanda.

Mrs. Thompson crossed to the door and turned to look at him. "I am not leaving this house until you and my daughter have spoken – even if I have to stay all night. I will not risk having you disappear again." Then she turned and left him.

Chapter 3

Patrick sat staring at his open door for some time. He read and reread the few paragraphs of the letter his mother had been writing to him just before she died. Why now? Why had his mother not attempted to share some of this information with him before now?

He tossed the letter on the desk. It was true he had asked her not to tell him about Amanda, but it was not as if she could not have slipped something in before now if she truly felt as this letter said *overwhelmed with the grief that his losing the lady who held his heart would bring him.*

He had not suddenly asked her about Amanda. And yet, she was writing to him about her! She could have ignored his request three years ago, but she did not. She had only done it now when she knew that Amanda would soon choose a husband and would never be his.

He shook his head and scowled at that letter. Now was not even the first time Amanda had almost been forever lost to him. According to his mother, Amanda had received an offer last year. Yet, his mother had not written to him about that!

There was only one reason that his confused and distraught mind could give for his mother never mentioning any of this to him before now – Mrs. Thompson. It had to be that Amanda's mother had not yet approved of him.

He rose and paced a circuit of the room. What had Mrs. Thompson said about that letter? After she read it, she knew he *needed* to read it?

Of course, she did!

His mother's words would be far more persuasive in putting Amanda forward to him than Mrs. Thompson's would be. And apparently now, thanks to the death of his brother, Patrick was finally acceptable. He was an estate owner, after all, and not just a mere second son, attempting to find his way in the world through some lowly profession. He blew out a frustrated breath and shook his head. He was only an estate owner if he chose to keep Ashmore Lodge, and, at the moment, he was not certain he cared to retain it or anything that would remind him of Amanda.

There was only one thing to do. He must go speak with Amanda. It was the only way he was going to rid his house of his mother's conniving friend. Then, he would drown his sorrows in a bottle of something, write a letter to his brother's solicitor regarding the disposal of his inheritance, and prepare the staff to accept a new master – one who did not bear the name Mullins.

Patrick descended the stairs and took two steps toward the library before retreating to the portrait gallery. As he walked along the length of the room, he stopped now and then to remember who the relations were who were staring back at him. It would be difficult to disappoint so many generations of Mullins, but what else was he to do? He could not stay here where he would be forced to see her. He would do a fine job of remembering how unworthy he was without the constant reminder.

He moved slowly, deliberately, reverently from one ancestor to the next until he came to the last portrait, the one of himself with his brother and their parents. As tears gathered in his eyes at the sight of the family he had lost, he attempted to push them aside by recalling just how tiring it had been to sit for that portrait and how his dear mother had borne his impatience so well. How he missed her!

This portrait would most certainly accompany him to his new home wherever that should be.

He turned and shook his head as he looked back down the gallery. He had hoped that this would be his home, that one day he would add a painting of his own family to this wall, but with a final sigh and a sharp pang of regret in his heart, he resigned himself to parting with Ashmore and disappointing all these ancestors whose likenesses hung here.

"I had heard you had returned," said Mrs. White, joining him in the gallery. "A day early, I might add."

Patrick tucked his morose mood away as best he could and chuckled at her teasing scold. He could tell she was not entirely put out to see him ahead of schedule. "I have always been impatient, have I not?"

"Oh, indeed," his housekeeper agreed most

readily, standing before the painting of Patrick's family. "But then, so was your father." She turned her head to look at him. "And yet, he was as fine a master as I ever had. I suspect you will be very much like him."

"I..." Patrick pressed his lips together, thinking better of what he wished to say. He could not disappoint her now. Not so soon after just arriving. "Thank you," he muttered instead before excusing himself to do what he did not wish to do but felt must be done.

"Miss Thompson," he said as he entered the library. She was sitting in his favourite chair, looking toward the garden doors, which were now hidden behind heavy drapes. It would be so easy for him to throw himself at her feet and ask her to be his, but he could not. For he had no desire to be accepted for his inheritance and nothing else.

"Your mother has insisted that we speak to one another," he continued, clasping his hands behind his back and standing as if he were giving an account to his colonel about some duty that had been completed. "However, I do not see a great need for a long, drawn-out discussion." He faltered as she turned toward him, and he saw her tear stained face. He dropped his gaze to look at the arm of the chair instead of her and willed his heart to stay strung together in some fashion rather than crumbling as it wished to do. "I must apologize for causing you pain, but it is for your own good."

He shook his head and turned from her. Those were nearly the same words she had said to him four years ago, and it hurt his heart as much now to say them as it had to hear them all that time ago.

"I will not be staying at Ashmore Lodge, so I fear I am not an acceptable choice for one such as yourself."

There. He had said it. And it sounded as hideous spoken aloud as it did when just a thought. His shoulders sagged, nearly unable to bear up under the strain of the task he had set before himself.

"Go to town as you planned. Find a husband worthy of you – one who will please your mother. I have never been and never will be that man."

Some of the anger from earlier began to return and his shoulders lifted. This was for the best. Supposing he had command of his sensibilities, he turned toward her and bowed.

"I thank you once again for preparing the house so well for my return. I do regret that I will not be staying longer than the few weeks necessary to see that all is in order to dispense of the estate."

With that, he left the room. It was cowardly of him not to give her an opportunity to respond, and he knew it. However, one did not stand around waiting for the enemy to retaliate when making a sneak attack, especially when one felt as vulnerable to surrender as he did within the intimacy of the dimly lit library. Exposing one's weakness was not among the lessons taught in how to win a battle. One made his strike and moved on to what needed to be done next. He could contemplate casualties and other such things when the campaign was over. For now, he needed to focus on his next objective of informing Mrs. Thompson that he had done as she requested. He had spoken to her daughter.

"Mrs. Thompson."

She looked up at him from where she sat near the hearth in the sitting room. "Have you spoken to Amanda already?"

He nodded. "I have. You will wish to take her home where she can recover from her disappointment in the comfort of familiar surroundings."

"I beg your pardon?" Mrs. Thompson looked at him aghast.

"I am not keeping Ashmore Lodge, Mrs. Thompson, and therefore, I will not be pursuing your daughter as I will not be the proper sort of husband she deserves."

It was much easier to speak of these things to Mrs. Thompson without his heart threatening to shatter, for the very sight of her aroused his disgust at having been tossed aside, only to be picked up again when what he possessed matched her desires for her daughter.

"What do you mean you are not keeping Ashmore Lodge?"

Patrick turned to find a wild-eyed Amanda at the door to the sitting room.

"Just that," he said as calmly as one could when faced on two sides by displeased women, "I am not keeping Ashmore. I am selling it. I had not thought to, but then, once I got here, I realized it would be for the best."

"For the best?" Amanda nearly shouted. "For whose best?"

He swallowed. "For mine."

The only thing about giving up his home that

was for his best was that it would allow him to live in some distant location far away from where he would have to be reminded of her and the family she would have.

"For Ashmore's," he added.

"How is it best for either you or the estate?" Amanda stomped toward him. "This place has been in your family for generations."

"Your mother would be disappointed," Mrs. Thompson added from her seat near the fire.

Her words turned his thoughts from sweeping Amanda into his arms and assuring her he would not leave to something more suiting to his purpose – bitterness.

"Yes, I will have to live with that knowledge," he said, turning toward Mrs. Thompson, while still keeping a watch on her daughter, "but then I am used to living with regret. I have had four years to practice, so adding my mother's displeasure to what I already carry should not be too difficult a thing to do. There is always the hope, I suppose, if I continue my career as an officer, that one of the skirmishes into which I am flung will rid me of the ability to feel regret. Not that I was so fortunate up to now."

That seemed to quell some of the anger he saw in Amanda's eyes while causing her mother to look horrified. Apparently, neither of them knew what destruction they had caused in his life.

"What do you mean you have not been fortunate?" Amanda asked.

"I am still alive," he replied flatly. He had never entered battle wishing to die some painful death at the end of a bayonet or from a musket's or cannon's ball, but there were moments when that pain had seemed more welcome than the pain he faced in remembering her.

"You wished to die?" Amanda moved toward a chair, her hand out in front of her as if she needed to feel her way to it.

"Often," he whispered.

She sank down onto the edge of a chair. "Because of me?"

He gave a sharp nod of his head. "But I wished more to see my mother again than to die, so I did my best to not be killed. However, now...well, there is not much reason left, is there?"

He turned away from her as she dissolved into tears, crossed to the window, and stared out into the blackness.

"No wonder you hate me," she said.

"I do not hate you," he said without turning toward her. "I love you as much now as I did four years ago."

"But I sent you away."

He shook his head. "No, your mother sent me away. It was her persuasion that did the job of parting me from both my mother and you."

"You did not have to sail to the Canadas!" Mrs. Thompson cried. "You could have studied the law or taken orders."

He laughed bitterly and turned from the window. "And be near enough to watch another more acceptable choice court and win the desire of my heart?" He shook his head. "I could not then, and I will not now. The Canadas are not so dreadful a place. Parts are actually quite civilized."

Mrs. Thompson rose from her seat and approached him. "But if you love her, why do you not attempt to win her?"

"Because she does not love me," he replied.

"But I do!" Amanda cried. "I have for years!"

Sorrow overwhelmed him as he shook his head. "I wish I could believe that."

"Why do you not?" Amanda asked.

"Why did your mother wish for me to read the letter left by my mother?"

Amanda's brows furrowed. "Perhaps because it was from your mother – it was her last words to you."

He turned toward the window again. "I also wish I could believe that, but I do not."

How he wished he could just believe that both Amanda and Mrs. Thompson welcomed him for him and not for his estate. Of Amanda's love, he could more readily convince his heart because he longed with every fiber of his being to be loved by her.

"Then what reason do you give it?"

There was no mistaking the anger in Mrs. Thompson's voice.

"I am now acceptable. My brother has died, and I am now acceptable. What greater feat would there be than to secure your daughter as the mistress of an estate so near to your home?" He shrugged. "It is brilliant maneuvering. However, I do not wish to be a pawn in some game. If you will excuse me, I have had a long day. I will not be fleeing Ashmore in the middle of the night, so you may attempt to work on me at some later time if you choose.

However, if you do not, I will understand." He bowed to Amanda. "I wish you well in your season. I hope you can find someone who is truly worthy of you."

How many times had he fled her presence now? He was not certain he wished to keep count, for, with each removal from her presence, his heart crumbled a little more. If only he could be assured of her love for him, if only he could see himself as worthy of her because of who he was and not because of an inheritance that had been thrust upon him, then – ah, then — he might finally find happiness.

Chapter 4

"Good morning, Sir," Mrs. White greeted Patrick as he passed her on his way to the breakfast room. "I believe you will find several choices to your liking." She entered the room behind him. "You will see the Cook has not forgotten your favourites."

Indeed, there were several items of food that he favoured sitting on the table near where his brother had always sat and his father before him. It should be his place now, but it would not be. Therefore, he moved the place setting to the first chair on the left. This is where he belonged. He was not claiming Ashmore. He did not deserve to sit in the place of its master.

Mrs. White arched a brow and wore a look of displeasure at his choice of seats.

He shifted his eyes to his plate as he sat down

and prepared to pour himself a cup of tea. He did not need Mrs. White's reproving looks to make him feel as lowly as a drunk passed out in the alleyway behind the Rose and Crown. He had spent a great deal of the night pondering how he was failing his family and the staff.

"Was there something you needed, Mrs. White?"

He had no desire to have her watch him not eat what had been explicitly prepared with him in mind. He was both grateful and touched by the remembrance of what he preferred and the effort to make his return feel more like a grand arrival than a necessity of tragedy. However, he had very little desire to do more than drink a cup of tea. His appetite was gone and having her standing before him, looking stern, was not helping it to return.

Before she could reply, there was a clattering in the corridor followed by a very feminine "Blast!"

"Who is that?" Patrick asked Mrs. White. He suspected he knew precisely who it was. Amanda had always favoured saying blast when things did not go as planned or she dropped one item or another.

"We have guests."

Patrick held Mrs. White's gaze, which did not waver. Was she going to tell him who his guests were? Or was she just going to stand there looking very much as his tutor had when the man discovered Patrick had hidden his ink?

As the sound of a discussion in the hall entered the breakfast room, his housekeeper finally spoke again. "Mrs. Thompson and her daughter stayed the night. I believe Mrs. Thompson is leaving now, but Miss Thompson will remain for the time being. I did not think you would mind if I lent them a few of your mother's items for sleeping so that their clothing could be presentable today."

He stared at her open-mouthed as she walked toward the door. He was correct. That blast had been from Amanda. But why was she here and not leaving?

"I could not turn Miss Thompson out when she was in the state she was in last evening after you retired to your room." Mrs. White stood mere feet from the door. "The last time I saw her looking so distressed was four years ago." She tipped her head and raised a brow once again. "I know I overstep my bounds, Sir, but seeing as I shall not be in your employ for long, I find the overstep does not bother me so very much."

He did not miss her meaning. She knew that he was not staying, and she was a great deal less than pleased. In fact, he was quite certain she was as angry as he had ever seen her. However, before he could plead that he was going to speak to her this morning, she continued.

"Four years ago, that young lady nearly died."

Patrick blinked. Amanda? Amanda had almost died?

"You will be polite to her and see to it that she eats. It was her lack of eating from the distress she felt at your hasty departure that made her susceptible to the illness which almost took her from us. You may remove yourself from those who care about you – for I assure you that many of us who have watched you grow over the years hold you in a special place in our hearts – but I, for one, will not tolerate your boyish behaviour causing us to lose Miss Thompson. She and her family have been a delight to serve when they visit."

With that and a fierce glare, Mrs. White did what Patrick was so adept at doing and left the room without giving him a moment to gather his thoughts and speak.

Patrick was still attempting to sort through what he had just heard when the second wave of attack entered the room, looking beautiful despite the dark circles that hung under her eyes. He pushed to his feet. "Good morning, Miss Thompson."

"Is it good, Mr. Mullins?" Her reply was cool, like the edge of a knife.

It appeared she had not lost her sharp tongue in four years. "It is what one says."

"One says much that one does not mean." She gave him a pointed look as she took the chair across from him and waited for a footman to bring her what she needed to eat.

"I should like to know what you mean by that, but Mrs. White has given me specific orders to remain polite and to see that you eat." He pushed a basket of muffins toward her. If he remembered correctly, a cup of tea and a muffin were her preference for breaking her fast.

Her lips tipped up at the corners as she took one of the muffins from the basket. "Are you not eating?" she asked, looking at his empty plate.

He shook his head. "I do not think I could if I tried."

"One should probably try so that one might prove the veracity of one's thoughts."

He shook his head and returned the smile she gave him. "Very well, I will try." He took a muffin, broke off a bit of it, and popped it into his mouth. It tasted of lightness and home for a moment until he remembered that he was not home and had to reach for his tea to wash down the ash the muffin had become. "I was correct." He pushed his plate away from him.

"I am sorry to hear it. Ashmore's cook usually produces very tasty food." She took a nibble of her muffin.

"It is not the quality of the food that is amiss."

"No? Then what is it?"

His eyes narrowed as she batted her lashes innocently. She knew exactly what was amiss. "I do not wish to leave Ashmore."

"Then do not leave." She put her muffin down and looked him in the eye, begging him to debate with her.

"I must not argue. Mrs. White would not be pleased."

"She is not pleased that you are leaving, so in for a penny, in for a pound as it were." Amanda leaned back with her cup of tea.

He shook his head. "I was going to tell her this morning."

Amanda shrugged one shoulder and sipped her tea, waiting for him to continue.

"Mrs. White said you were staying with us for some time?"

She nodded and smiled.

"How long are you planning to remain at Ashmore?"

She shook her head and placed her cup on the table. "I believe you said you would be here for the few weeks it took to complete the disposal of your inheritance or some such thing, so I cannot tell you more precisely than what you have told me. However, it would be greatly appreciated if you would give me at least a day's warning before we are to relocate to wherever it is we are going."

Patrick reached for his tea, hoping that a sip of it would help his heart return to where it belonged instead of blocking his throat and hammering in his ears. She was planning to leave with him?

She smiled, broke off the tiniest bit of muffin and rose from her seat.

"You have not finished eating." Those were not the words he really wished to say, but in a panic, he blurted whatever he had to so that she would not quit the room until she had explained herself.

"I am not leaving." She had come around the table to where he sat and patted him on the shoulder before continuing down the length of the room to the windows at its far end. "The frost fairies were busy last night," she said, glancing back to where he sat. "Their decorations are so beautiful in the first light of morning. See how they sparkle?"

The frosty designs on the window were not the only thing to sparkle. The sun glinted off the copper of her hair and framed her face in light.

"Are the designs as beautiful in Canada?" She beckoned for him to join her at the window.

He shook his head. She was not going to let him ignore her. "I have sketches of a few."

"I should like to see them." She sighed. "It is a pity you had to transport all your things to England only to have to return them to Canada when you leave again. We are going to Canada, are we not? It sounded as though that was what you planned when you spoke to Mother and me last night."

"At the risk of starting an argument and incurring more of the wrath of Mrs. White, why do you keep saying *we* are going?"

She blew on the window allowing it to fog up with her breath, then with a finger traced a heart in it. "My mother disapproves of me writing on the window like this."

"Your mother disapproves of many things." He was one of those things.

"Not so much as she used to," Amanda blew on the window again before tracing another heart on the pane. "She has agreed to allow me to go to Canada with you. She was not happy about it, but I would not be moved. I reminded her that you have established yourself in a profession just as she required four years ago before giving me her blessing to marry. Never had she once mentioned that you must live close to Kympton or Lambton or anywhere in Derbyshire for that matter. If you had taken up a different profession, I would have been moved to wherever it was that you practiced law or found a parish."

She turned toward him. "I do not care where you live or what you are as long as you are my husband. I will not live another day with my heart torn in half. I will not, Patrick. I simply will not."

Patrick shook his head and blinked. He turned toward the window and then back toward her. Was she saying what he thought she was saying?

"Mother has gone home to prepare my things for travel. Later today, she will, of course, send what I need for my stay here, but the rest should be crated up and delivered to Ashmore before you have made all the arrangements necessary to sell the place. I can help you with anything that needs to be organized or listed or the like." She was talking rapidly as she did when she was nervous.

"I do not know what tasks the selling of a home entails, but I am a quick learner and need only to be instructed. Then, when Mr. Dobney has called the banns, we shall marry, and everything will be all properly ready for our departure. No, not quite. Mother has a sister in town who is rattling about her townhouse and either she can come to live with Mother or Mother can go to live with her." She blew once more on the window and began to make another heart. "Then, all shall be ready – as soon as Mother is settled with someone to keep her company."

He saw her lips quiver, and she blinked rapidly. She was willing to leave all that she knew and loved for him – no matter what his profession, no matter if he owned an estate or not – she was choosing him. And while the thought elated him, it also made him feel quite small for having questioned her motives.

He grasped the hand that was closest to him. "You still wish to marry me? After all these years? After last night?"

She nodded. "I am foolish like that."

He smiled. Anyone else would have said a simple yes, but not his sharp-tongued Amanda. She would remind him of his idiocy while still accepting him.

"I have never intended not to marry you," she added. "But my mother was right four years ago. We were not truly ready to marry. How would you have supported me, let alone a child? It was imprudent to think that we could survive on just the interest from my dowry and your allowance." She took his other hand, and they stood facing each other.

"That is what I attempted to tell you, but you did not hear me." She blinked against tears, but one escaped and slid down her cheek.

"All you heard was my rejection. I could see it in your eyes. I have seen it in your eyes so many times when I have closed mine. Please, say you will have me. That I have not driven you away forever."

"Will you have me even if I do not sell Ashmore?"

"Only if you believe me when I say that I would have you even without it. I wish only to be by your side wherever you are." Her lips tipped up on one side. "I do require now, as I did four years ago, that we be able to live comfortably enough to feed and house our children and employ a servant or two because to begin a family with less would, in my opinion, be – "

"Imprudent," he finished. "As is selling my inheritance if there is no reason to escape the pain of seeing you wed to another." He drew and released a breath that took from him the last remnants of the heaviness which had settled into his soul upon realizing, yesterday, that he must leave both Ashmore and Amanda.

"I am likely not good enough for you, but if you

will have me, and if you will be content to be the mistress of Ashmore, then I shall daily endeavour to prove myself worthy of you. Will you forgive me for my foolishness and agree to be my wife? For I like you, have no desire to live my life with half a heart, and mine needs you to be complete."

She dropped his hands and turned toward the window where she blew on the glass, traced a heart in the fog, and quickly scrawled *yes* before the vapour vanished.

When she turned toward him, he pulled her into his arms. His heart beat wildly in his chest. From tragedy and the deepest cold hopelessness, a soul could feel, had arisen something of great beauty, something that he did not deserve, something that he would cherish for all time.

"I love you, Amanda." He pulled back to smile down at her. "I have always loved you for as long as I can remember, even when I was pulling your hair and teasing you with frogs, and I will love you for infinitely longer."

She reached a hand up to stroke his cheek. "Until the frost fairies forget to paint on the windowpanes of Ashmore in the winter?"

He looked up toward the ceiling. It was

excessively unmanly to cry, but even rolling his eyes upward or blinking could not keep his tears from falling.

"Even longer than that," he answered. Then, he captured her lips with his and attempted to pour every ounce of his love into that kiss.

Four years of separation overtook them. His hands roamed up and down her back hungrily, tugging her closer and closer to him while her hands knotted themselves in his hair, holding him, so that he could not help but kiss her long and deep as their lips parted and their tongues tangled. She was delicious, and she was his – finally, she was his. He broke their kiss and rested his forehead on hers.

"You should not stay here until we are married." There was no way he was going to make it to the altar without anticipating his vows if she remained under the same roof as him. As it was, it was likely going to be a difficult battle during the day when she was visiting.

"I was serious about never being parted from you again," she replied. "I am not leaving."

"I do not trust myself," he admitted. "If we are alone..."

She kissed his lips lightly, and he saw a spark of amusement in his eyes. "My mother does not trust you either, and so she will also be staying here until we marry."

Patrick groaned. He would have to speak to Philip to see how quickly a license could be readied and arrangements could be made.

"She is not here now," Amanda said suggestively. "Although, there are footmen present so do not do more than kiss me."

He bent his head to capture her lips again and kissed her to the edge of his resolve. Then, once again he rested his forehead against hers.

"We should speak with Mrs. White," Amanda said. "And Philip and his brother Marcus are bringing some greenery – bows and such. We intended to keep them outside the servants' entrance until next week when we will shake the snow off them and place a few around the sitting room and dining room." She wrapped her arm around his and laid her head against his shoulder as they moved away from the window. "I know it is not proper to be too festive, but I think it is what your mother would have wanted. She did so love

Christmas. Oh!" her head popped up. "We must also get a yule log."

He chuckled. "We will do all of those things." He stopped at the table. "But not until you have eaten as per Mrs. White's orders." He kissed her forehead and then held her chair for her.

"I shall only eat if you do." She wrinkled her nose as she tasted her tea. "We shall need fresh cups. It has grown cold."

Patrick motioned to one of the footmen who was still standing at his post. Then, he moved his things to the head of the table – the proper place for the master of Ashmore to take — before tucking himself into his chair and enjoying the most wonderful breakfast he had ever tasted as he listened to Amanda tell him story upon story about all that had happened in Derbyshire while he had been gone.

He was home. Never to leave again. He was exactly where he was meant to be. Here. With her. Until the frost fairies never returned to paint another windowpane in winter. Or perhaps even longer.

Before You Go

If you enjoyed this book, be sure to let others
know by leaving a review.

~*~*~

Want to know when other books in this series
will be available?
You can always know what's new with my
books by subscribing to my mailing list.
(There will, of course, be a thank you gift for
joining because I think my readers are awesome!)
Book News from Leenie Brown
(bit.ly/LeenieBBookNews)

~*~*~

Turn the page to read an excerpt from another
one of Leenie's books

First Blooms and
Second Chances
Excerpt

Below is the first chapter of "A Lily in Midwinter" which is the fourth novelette in *First Blooms and Second Chances*, Nature's Fury and Delights, Volume 2.

CHAPTER 1

And so it begins. We must leave in a fortnight, and Mother has had the modiste to the house twice just this week to alter my gowns. There was no need for it. They fit just fine. However, she is convinced that a few more embellishments or a little less room to breath will help them make me more desirable to some quizzing glass-carrying fop.

Frederick Bartholomew George looked at the

directions on the front of the rain dampened letter a second time. Those smudges definitely looked as if they were his address, but the letter was most certainly not meant for him. According to the address on the front, it was meant for an S. G– *something.* Rain and ink were not friends. What one attempted to make clear, the other washed away. Perhaps there was a name in the letter which would give some indication as to for whom this letter was intended.

That is not fair of me to count all gentlemen as peacocks, but you know how it is. Mama has her ideas about what constitutes an acceptable husband, which, you know full well, are not the same as mine.

Oh, Sally, I am torn. I want so much to see you, but I dread our visit to your home for it will mark the end of a pleasant autumn of books and unchaperoned walks and the beginning of a trying season filled with 'stand tall', 'smile', 'my is he not the most handsome gentleman you have ever seen', and the like.

Please write and assure me that all will be well, and that I will be able to weather the machinations of my mother long enough to find a suitable husband. I have no time to write more, for we must be off at once to secure some ghastly concoction from the milliner. (It will be lovely, I am sure. However, at present, I am very ill-disposed to liking much of anything.)

I send my love to you and yours.

Yours affectionately,

Lily

Sally? He searched his memory for any gently bred young lady he knew who was called Sally. Sadly, he could not think of one. If he knew who she was, he would send this letter to her straightaway. However, all he knew was that he was not Sally, and Miss Lily Whoever-She-Was would not be receiving a letter in reply to calm her nerves about her mother's matchmaking ways. Unless...

He put the letter on his desk and leaned back in his chair. There was a return address. He could inform Miss Lily that her letter had been delivered to the wrong person. Recognizing that this was likely the best idea, he opened his writing box, took out a pen, and uncapped his ink. He drew a line under Miss Lily's closing remarks and began to write.

Dear Miss Lily,

(Forgive me, but there was no surname attached to your signature and the name on the outside of the letter

was smudged. I am afraid it has been dreadfully rainy lately, and it is preventing me from being more formal in my address.)

It is my regrettable task to inform you that your letter has not reached its intended destination and has, instead, landed on my desk amongst a pile of papers. I thank you for the diversion your missive has provided, and I wish to express my condolences regarding your mother. I know some of what you face, for I also have a mother, as well as a sister, who are both anxious to see me married. However, I willingly admit that my being a gentleman does put me at somewhat of an advantage, though only marginally, as my mother is a terrific schemer.

I am returning this to you in hopes that your friend will eventually receive your news and that she might send you her assurances.

Sincerely and with best wishes for your impending travels and season,

F.B. George

There. He read Miss Lily's letter once again and chuckled at the seeming disparity between mother and daughter. Then, he reread his own. It was brief and friendly. Not at all stiff and business-like. He had tried to keep it in a tone which he might use if writing to his sister or his good friend. From what he could see, he had succeeded. Confident that there should not be a thing for Miss Lily to find wrong with his note, he sealed it and had it posted before returning to the much less interesting estate matters which still remained on his desk

~*~*~

"I heard Flitcroft instructing a footman to see something sent by express." Frederick's mother kept her eyes on her dinner plate and meticulously cut her venison into tiny pieces while she pried into her son's life.

"A letter was misdirected, and I wished to have it returned as quickly as possible." The roasted celeriac was particularly good this evening, nearly as tasty as the mushrooms in butter sauce. Nearly, but not quite.

"Who was it for?" His younger sister's fork on which was skewered both a slice of venison and a mushroom hung just over her plate as she turned to her attention to her brother.

She was far too curious by half, in his opinion, and his mother did little to curb such behaviour. In fact, his mother was looking just as expectantly at him as his sister was.

"The directions were somewhat spoiled by the rain."

"You could not make them out at all?" She finally popped her bite of food into her mouth. He should be free from questions from her for a minute or two.

He shook his head. "The names were the worse for the wear, I am afraid. The person for whom the letter was intended has the initials S.G. That is all I know other than the sender's name is Lily."

"Lily?" A curious look passed between his mother and sister. "That is a very pretty name, do you not think, Rosalie?"

"Simply lovely. I would imagine the lady who bears such a name to be quite delicate, much like this cup." She lifted her teacup and took a sip.

Why she refused to have wine with her meal, he did not know. But she did. It was always tea with dinner and wine with a bit of something sweet later. It was completely against how things should be done if you asked him.

"See how it is so delicately painted?" She held the cup in his direction. "There not a garish flower on here. Just simple rosebuds twining around each other in a field of white, bordered by a golden band."

Roses were a favourite in his family, and all the cups and saucers in this particular set of dishes paid homage to his grandmother's favourite flower.

"She did not sound delicate," Frederick muttered, returning to his delightful mushrooms. His sister could be so fanciful.

"What did you say, Freddie?" Rosalie skewered her brother with a pointed look.

"I said that she did not sound delicate," he repeated as he attempted to avoid both his sister's and his mother's raised brows. "I read the letter," he admitted.

"You did what?"

He winced at his mother's sharp tone.

"I know that it is rude to read someone else's correspondence, and yet it was necessary."

It was also rude to read the words written in a journal which was not his, and it was beyond the pale to stand close enough to someone's shoulder so that he could read a letter as it was being written. How many times had his curious nature won him that lecture as a child?

"I was looking to see if I could discover to whom the letter was addressed so that I might find its rightful owner. It was intended for some lady named Sally. That is all I know."

"No, it is not all you know," Rosalie said, her lips were pursed with displeasure when he looked at her. "You said Lily did not sound delicate, and there must be a reason for such disparagement of a lady you do not even know."

"I was not disparaging," he defended.

"You said she was not delicate."

"Exactly." That was not a disparagement. It was a statement of observation. And there was, in his mind, absolutely nothing wrong with being considered *not delicate*. In fact, if he were pushed to be blunt, he'd rather have a lady who was *not delicate*.

"Delicate means easily broken. Miss Lily did not sound easily broken."

She sounded rather as if she might be capable of withstanding a great deal of disagreeableness with just a sardonic word and a roll of her eyes. The thought brought a smile to his lips. He might like to meet this Lily.

"A lady may be delicate *and* strong," his mother

cautioned, drawing his mind back to the conversation at hand rather than allowing him to continue imagining Miss Lily. "A teacup holds very hot water without so much as a whimper of complaint. Fine features and manners do not indicate a lack of fortitude."

Frederick sighed, loudly, purposefully, and with a look of exasperation for his mother. "I am certain that is true. Could we please not make this into a lesson on what I should be looking for in a wife?"

His mother batted her lashes and smiled. "Would I do that?"

"Yes. And it would likely come with a list of ladies whom you think I should court."

"You are not getting any younger."

"Thank you, Mother. I had forgotten," he retorted wryly.

She was laughing at him behind her wine goblet. He could tell by the way her eyes were dancing. She did like to tease him about his need to marry.

"Since I am nearly thirty – it is only three years away as you might remember – perhaps I should just propose to the next lady who enters our door."

"I would not be opposed to that." His mother

smirked at him as she returned her glass to the table.

That was not the response he had hoped for from his mother. She was supposed to tell him that he was being foolish or some such thing. The eyebrow over his left eye arched.

"Are we expecting guests?"

"It is nearly Christmas," his mother said.

How had he forgotten? His mother always entertained at Christmas. Of course, there would be guests. Their period of mourning was over. The thought was sobering and tinged with sadness.

"A dear friend of mine from my school years is coming to visit. We see each other each year in town during the season – when I am there. At one time, she visited here on a regular basis, but, with how busy life gets as one's children get older, it has been years since she has visited Rose Hall.

"However, her youngest daughter is to take in the season in town this year, and since our estate is closer to London than theirs is and could very well be her last year to be required to take in the season, it seemed a good plan to have her visit on her way." She took a sip from her wine glass. "Her husband will join us, but not until she and her daughter have been here for a fortnight."

"Will it not be fabulously grand to have so many around our table for the Christmas feast this year?" His sister was far too excited.

"I take it you know who these people are?"

Rosalie's head bobbed up and down. "I have met the daughter, and we get on famously."

"But this is the daughter's first time in town for the season, is it not? How have you met her?"

"One can be in town for reasons other than the season."

He scowled at her. That was not a very good explanation.

"Her older sister just married this past June," Rosalie said. "Now, it is her turn. She has been in town but not part of the season proper on account of her sister."

He nodded. That made sense. It was not unusual for only one daughter to be presented at a time in order to put her at as good an advantage as possible in securing a husband.

"Do these people have a name?" He should likely know who would be arriving at his house. His mother was usually good about informing him of these details, and that she had not was excessively suspicious.

"Of course, they do, silly," his sister replied before taking up her teacup once again and deigning to not tell him anything further.

He looked to his mother. "Would someone please share this tidbit of information with me? I should like to know who I will be hosting."

"Do you really need to know it?" Rosalie asked.

"Yes." Why would he not need to know the name of his guests?

"The family name is Brinson," his mother answered, causing Rosalie to roll her eyes as if displeased that such information had been shared.

"And it is just Mrs. Brinson, Miss Brinson, and eventually Mr. Brinson who will be spending the yuletide with us?"

"Yes." His mother sighed. "Your father enjoyed having guests."

Frederick settled back into his chair. He wished his father was still here to see to all the guests and festivities at Rose Hall. However, he was not and had not been for what would be two years come spring. Frederick was not as at ease with guests as his father had been. He was more likely than not to inadvertently cause offense.

"I will do my best," he assured his mother.

She smiled. "I know you will. Just be yourself, and they will have to love you."

He doubted that. His mother had a far rosier opinion of him than most did. To her, he could do very little wrong – other than refusing to consider marrying one of her many suggestions, that is.

"I agree." Rosalie was smiling as if she knew a secret. "And you must believe me because I barely tolerate you many days." She batted her lashes.

He chuckled. "I should hate to see how cossetted I would be if you found me more than tolerable." This, as expected, drew a laugh from both his mother and sister. They were two ladies cut from the same clothe. Two very lovely ladies.

"Wait. You are not attempting to match me with Miss Brinson, are you?"

"No!" they both replied almost too quickly. He would have to be on his guard.

"Did we not promise we would not meddle after that fiasco two years ago? I truly did not know Miss White was such a harridan, or I would not have pushed her at you," his mother said.

His mother had been terrifically apologetic when it came to light that the lady she was championing as the best choice of the season had a foul temper and razor-sharp tongue which she used to slice apart anyone who did not do as she thought they should. The lady hid it well enough in public, unless she thought that her prize, which happened to be him at the time, was being snatched from her.

"Yes, you did promise," he agreed, "but I know how you both are."

"It would not be so bad if you were to like Miss Brinson," Rosalie admitted. "Not that I am suggesting you should. I am only assuring you that if you do, I will not feel as if you are attempting to steal my friend from me, and I can assure you that she is in no way a harridan."

"I will keep that in mind." They might say they were not meddling, but he was nearly positive they were. But what could be done, save to be vigilant?

He looked from one to the other of the ladies he held dear. "Very well, I shall pretend to believe you." He rose from his chair.

"Are you not going to stay for dessert?" his mother asked. "It is carrot cake."

Frederick paused at the door. Carrot cake was

on his list of favourite sweet indulgences. "Perhaps you could send a piece to me in my study?"

"Are you going to hide from us all evening?" his sister asked. "I had hoped to play a game or two."

He smiled at his sister. "If I can have carrot cake while adding that final column of numbers and a glass of Madeira when I join you, then I shall play whatever you wish." He held up a finger. "As long as the game does not end with me being married."

"I have no idea what you have against marrying," she called after him.

He had nothing against the institution of marriage. He just needed to find the right lady, and that, to this point in his life, remained the sticking point.

Acknowledgements

There are many who have had a part in the creation of these stories. My critique buddies have read and commented on it. My editors have proofread for grammatical errors and plot holes. My boys and husband have not read the story and most likely never will. However, their encouragement and belief in my ability, as well as their patience when I became cranky or when supper was late or the groceries ran low, was invaluable.

And so, I would like to say *thank you* to Zoe, Rose, Betty, Kristine, Ben, and Kyle. I feel blessed through your help, support, and understanding.

I have not listed my dear husband in the above group because, to me, he deserves his own special thank you, for without his somewhat pushy insistence that I start sharing my writing, none of my writing goals and dreams would have been met.

Other Leenie B Books

You can find all of Leenie's books at this link
bit.ly/LeenieBBooks
where you can explore the collections below

~*~

Other Pens, Mansfield Park

~*~

Touches of Austen Collection

~*~

Dash of Darcy and Companions Collection

~*~

Marrying Elizabeth Series

~*~

Willow Hall Romances

~*~

The Choices Series

~*~

Darcy Family Holidays

~*~

Darcy and... An Austen-Inspired Collection

About the Author

Leenie Brown has always been a girl with an active imagination, which, while growing up, was both an asset, providing many hours of fun as she played out stories, and a liability, when her older sister and aunt would tell her frightening tales. At one time, they had her convinced Dracula lived in the trunk at the end of the bed she slept in when visiting her grandparents!

Although it has been years since she cowered in her bed in her grandparents' basement, she still has an imagination, which occasionally runs away with her, and she feeds it now as she did then — by reading!

Her heroes, when growing up, were authors, and the worlds they painted with words were (and still are) her favourite playgrounds! Now, as an adult, she spends much of her time in the Regency world, playing with the characters from her favourite Jane Austen novels and those of her own creation.

When she is not traipsing down a trail in an attempt to keep up with her imagination, Leenie resides in the beautiful province of Nova Scotia with her two sons and her very own Mr. Brown (a wonderful mix of all the best of Darcy, Bingley, and Edmund with a healthy dose of the teasing Mr. Tilney and just a dash of the scolding Mr. Knightley).

Connect with Leenie

E-mail:
LeenieBrownAuthor@gmail.com
Facebook:
www.facebook.com/LeenieBrownAuthor
Blog:
leeniebrown.com
Patreon:
https://www.patreon.com/LeenieBrown
Subscribe to Leenie's Mailing List:
Book News from Leenie Brown
(bit.ly/LeenieBBookNews)

www.ingramcontent.com/pod-product-compliance
Lightning Source LLC
Chambersburg PA
CBHW061324200626
46813CB00017B/2837